Evangeline came toward him, holding Ella on her hip.

"Hey, everything okay?" Denny asked.

She nodded, giving him a quick smile that didn't help his resolve much. The more time he spent with this woman, the harder it became to keep aloof from her. To remind himself that he wasn't the person for her.

She looked past him to the gathered herd. "Those calves look too young for yearlings," she said.

"I bought Bart's herd. A bit ahead of my five-year plan, but then my plan is in shreds right about now anyway."

Evangeline's expression shifted into a slow, careful smile. "So you planned to settle down."

"Eventually."

"I see."

As their eyes held he felt as if her bright smile dove into his soul and settled there. He drew in a cleansing breath and put his elbows up on the fence, his arm brushing hers. Neither moved away, and as their eyes met once again, Denny wondered, could something be happening between them?

Did he dare let it?

Books by Carolyne Aarsen

Love Inspired

*A Family-Style Christmas
 Yuletide Homecoming
 A Bride at Last
 The Cowboy's Bride
*A Mother at Heart
*A Family at Last
 A Hero for Kelsey
 Twin Blessings
 Toward Home
 Love Is Patient
 A Heart's Refuge
 Brought Together by Baby
 A Silence in the Heart
 Any Man of Mine
 Finally a Family
 A Family for Luke
 The Matchmaking Pact

Close to Home
Cattleman's Courtship
Cowboy Daddy
The Baby Promise
†The Rancher's Return
 The Cowboy's Lady
†Daddy Lessons
†Healing the Doctor's Heart
†Homecoming Reunion
†Catching Her Heart
‡A Father's Promise
‡Unexpected Father

*Stealing Home
†Home to Hartley Creek
‡Hearts of Hartley Creek

CAROLYNE AARSEN

and her husband, Richard, live on a small ranch in northern Alberta, where they have raised four children and numerous foster children, and are still raising cattle. Carolyne crafts her stories in an office with a large west-facing window through which she can watch the changing seasons while struggling to make her words obey.

Unexpected Father
Carolyne Aarsen

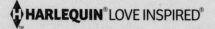

HARLEQUIN® LOVE INSPIRED®

Recycling programs
for this product may
not exist in your area.

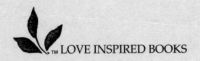 ™ LOVE INSPIRED BOOKS

ISBN-13: 978-0-373-81745-0

UNEXPECTED FATHER

Copyright © 2014 by Carolyne Aarsen

All rights reserved. Except for use in any review, the reproduction or utilization of this work in whole or in part in any form by any electronic, mechanical or other means, now known or hereafter invented, including xerography, photocopying and recording, or in any information storage or retrieval system, is forbidden without the written permission of the editorial office, Love Inspired Books, 233 Broadway, New York, NY 10279 U.S.A.

This is a work of fiction. Names, characters, places and incidents are either the product of the author's imagination or are used fictitiously, and any resemblance to actual persons, living or dead, business establishments, events or locales is entirely coincidental.

This edition published by arrangement with Love Inspired Books.

® and TM are trademarks of Love Inspired Books, used under license. Trademarks indicated with ® are registered in the United States Patent and Trademark Office, the Canadian Trade Marks Office and in other countries.

www.Harlequin.com

Printed in U.S.A.

The Lord is good to those whose hope is in Him,
to the one who seeks Him.

—*Lamentations* 3:25

I'd like to thank Captain Jeff Deptuck,
a real-life fireman, for his donation in the auction
to the Stollery Children's hospital that bought him a
role in the Hearts of Hartley Creek series.
Thanks for keeping us and our families safe.

Chapter One

"How could you doubt me, Lady Maria?" Lord Cavanaugh's dark gaze held a gleam of mirth, belying his gruff words.

Evangeline leaned her elbow on the bookstore's counter, licked her finger and turned the page of her book, releasing a satisfied smile at the perfect scene with the perfect hero.

"I made myself clear that no sacrifice is too great for you," he said, pulling her close. Maria's fan dropped to the floor. Ignoring the shocked looks of the other patrons of Almacks Assembly, Maria threw her arms around Lord Cavanaugh's neck, sharing a kiss with the only man she knew she could ever love.

Evangeline's long, wavy hair fell across the side of her face as she closed the book with a satisfied sigh and smoothed her hand over the cover, admiring the hero pictured on the front. His hair was artfully tousled; his cutaway coat perfectly emphasized his broad shoulders. He looked cultured and noble and suave and heroic.

Someday my own prince will come, she thought.

The chiming of bells from the door of her store broke into her reverie.

A man, silhouetted by the sun behind him, paused inside the frame. Tall, with broad shoulders, lean hips. Her heart skipped for a moment.

Then she saw the cowboy hat he wore.

Wrong genre.

Evangeline straightened, ready to take care of her first customer of the day.

"Are you Evangeline Arsenau?" the cowboy asked. His deep voice smooth as dark chocolate and Evangeline couldn't stop a languid sigh and a quickening of her heart.

"That's me," she said, wishing she didn't sound so breathless. She blamed her reaction on the book she was reading and the hero it depicted. The kind of man she'd been looking for all her life.

As she slipped the book under the counter, the man in the doorway stepped farther into the store and came into focus.

His shabby plaid shirt had seen better days years ago as had his once-white T-shirt. His faded and torn blue jeans were ragged at the hem where they met unlaced leather work boots so scuffed and stained she was unsure of the original color. He pulled his hat off his head, revealing mussed, overlong hair, and as he came near, she caught a hint of the too-familiar scent of diesel fumes.

Truck driver, she thought. *Cowboy truck driver.*

And Evangeline's foolish heart, which had only moments ago fluttered in anticipation at his silhouette, thudded in her chest.

Not a chance.

"I'm Denny Norquest," he said, holding a hand out to her, his smile showing even teeth white against the dark stubble shading his firm chin. "Your father told me to stop by Hartley Creek and say hello as I was heading to British Columbia. And here I am."

She frowned as her slender fingers were engulfed in his large hand. As expected, it was callused and rough, but enfolded hers in a firm grip. His dark eyes held hers as his well-shaped mouth lifted in a crooked smile.

For some silly reason her heart gave another flutter. Then his words registered.

"Hi? From my father?"

"Yeah. Andy said for me to tell you he was sorry he couldn't come like he said."

"Not coming?" She stared at Denny as the import of his words settled into her mind. "But he said... He promised... He was going to—" She clamped her lips on the words of disappointment and dismay that threatened to spill out.

"He said he would call you in a day or so," Denny continued when Evangeline didn't—or rather, couldn't—finish her sentence. "He also asked me to tell you to reschedule the visit to the lawyer to talk about the bookstore."

Every word coming out of Mr. Denny Norquest's mouth scattered Evangeline's carefully laid plans like dead leaves in a fall storm.

"So he's not coming," she repeated, trying to create some intelligent response.

"Not yet."

Evangeline could only nod, her disappointment morphing into anger. Anger that her father had so casually decided to change months of plans. Anger that he hadn't had the decency to break the news to her face.

Andy Arsenau was to arrive Monday, the day after tomorrow, to do what he had promised for so many years. Sign the bookstore he had inherited from his wife over to Evangeline.

She had planned the changes she'd wanted to make to the bookstore for months, pouring her time and energy into her ideas. She'd gotten in touch with contractors. More importantly, she had made an appointment with Zach Truscott, a lawyer in Hartley Creek and fiancée of her best friend, Renee, to finalize the deal.

She folded her arms over her chest and looked Mr. Norquest straight in the eye.

"Thank you for passing on the message. Is there anything else I can do for you?" she asked, trying mightily to stifle her anger. It wasn't this cowboy's fault her father had deigned to use him as his spokesperson.

But still…

"I didn't come here to only deliver that message." Denny continued, "The main reason I'm here is 'cause your dad said he has a place that you rent out sometimes."

Again Evangeline could only stare at Mr. Norquest, trying to follow where he led.

He stared back as he worked his cowboy hat around in his hands.

"He said something about an apartment in the back of the store I could stay in until then," Denny continued.

"The…the apartment here?" She poked her thumb over her shoulder, indicating the living quarters across the hall attached to the back of the store.

The living quarters where her father always

stayed when he was between jobs and between schemes. Trouble was, there was always another job. Always another scheme, so he never stayed long.

"Yeah. Your dad said I could stay here until I can move onto the ranch."

"Move…move onto the ranch?"

Her mind whirled as she fought to put his words into a place that made sense, trying to catch up to what he was saying. Now she knew what Alice felt like tumbling down the rabbit hole. "I thought after the renters moved out of the ranch house my dad would be—" She stopped herself from finishing that sentence.

Moving back onto the ranch. Just as he had said he would in the text he had sent her.

Evangeline pressed her hands on the sales counter, as if anchoring herself while she stumbled through this confusing conversation.

"He didn't say anything about moving onto the ranch. He's leasing it to me. For a five-year term." Denny's deep voice held an edge of impatience. "He said that the other renter's lease on the pasture was up and he wasn't renewing it."

The previous lessee wasn't renewing the lease because Evangeline's father had promised when he was finished his current job he would come back to Hartley Creek, sign the store over to her and settle on the ranch.

Make a home here. Be the father he hadn't been since her mother had died when Evangeline was eight.

The close call he'd had with his truck a couple of months ago was a wake-up for him to change his life. To find a meaning and purpose.

When he'd told Evangeline this, she had allowed a faint hope to bloom. The hope that he would finally be the father he hadn't been for most of her life. And that he would complete the unfinished deal on the bookstore she'd been managing for him for the past nine years. The bookstore he kept promising he would sign over to her.

"Did he say when he was coming back?"

Denny shrugged, slapping his hat against his thigh as if impatient to be done with her and her questions about her father.

"Andy said he would call and that in the meantime you have power of attorney over the ranch and that you would take care of things for me."

Evangeline felt the last faint hope die with Denny's decisive words. Her father probably wasn't coming at all. She might never own this bookstore or have a father who wanted to be with her.

"Every time," Evangeline muttered, her hands curling into fists. "He gets me every time."

Then, to her dismay, her voice broke and she felt her eyes prickle. She turned aside, grabbed a tissue and dabbed at her eyes, hoping, praying, she didn't smear her mascara, to boot.

She stared at the door at the back of the store leading to her father's apartment, swallowing a stew of anger and grief at the timing of her father's news. It didn't help that this came on the heels of yet another disappointment.

Two months ago her boyfriend of two years, Tyler, had said he needed a break, promising Evangeline they would get back together again. A few days later Evangeline had seen him driving his bright red sports car with a young blonde cozied up at his side, her arms wrapped around him.

Some break.

And now it looked as though her father was backing out on his promise, too.

Then, thankfully, the door bells rang, announcing the presence of a customer as Larissa Beck entered the store. Finally an excuse to get away from this situation for a few minutes. Catch her breath. Center herself.

As Evangeline excused herself, she stifled her disappointment to the blow her father had dealt her yet one more time.

When would she learn?

Evangeline had grown up on the ranch Denny was talking about. The best time of her life, spent with her mother and her father and wide-open spaces. Then, when she'd turned eight, her mother had died and her world shifted and changed. She and her father had stayed at the ranch for a month and then he got a job driving a truck. He'd made arrangements to lease out the ranch and taken Evangeline to the bookstore where her mother's sister lived. Auntie Josie had agreed to take care of her for a while, and he had promised to be back once the job was done.

And this became his constant refrain each time he blew back into town with the spring thaw and his pockets full of cash. Each time he came back he made Evangeline think he was staying put. But he'd grow restless and his eyes would glaze over whenever she'd made plans for the store. Two or three or sometimes four months later he'd head out again, looking for another adventure, another challenge. Another business to invest in.

Now this…truck driver slash cowboy, a man she didn't even know, had delivered another blow to her future plans with no more emotion than an announcer delivering the weather forecast.

And her father hadn't even had the decency to give her the news face-to-face.

"So who's the rough, tough character by the till?" Larissa asked when Evangeline joined her.

"Friend of my father's. No one important."

When Larissa lifted one eyebrow at her dismissive tone, Evangeline felt a nudge of regret. It wasn't Denny's fault he had come as her absent father's mouthpiece.

Didn't mean she had to like it, though.

No one important.

Well, that was probably true, Denny thought, dropping his hat onto his head, watching Evangeline as she walked—no, swayed—toward the customer. Though Andy had showed him a picture of his daughter, Denny hadn't been prepared for her effect in real life.

Tall, willowy, her long dark hair spilling in curly waves over her shoulders. Her tilted smile and the way her green eyes curved up at the corners combined to make her look as if she held some curious secret that would make you laugh if she told you.

"Cute as a button," her father had described her. His own beautiful little princess tucked away in her own little tower. Andy had told Denny that she lived above the bookstore.

Denny glanced around the building with its old-fashioned high ceilings and heavy-beamed wood trim. The large front windows flanking the door spilled light into a store chock-full of bookshelves weighted with paperbacks, hardcovers, picture books, kids' books....

He was never much of a reader and it made him nervous to see so many books packed into one place. But he could picture Evangeline here. She looked exactly like the princess Andy always talked about with such fondness.

Evangeline laughed at something her customer said as they walked to the cash register, the customer's arms full of books.

"You'll like this book, Larissa," Evangeline said as she rang up her customer's purchases. "I'm thinking of suggesting it for book club. You coming?"

"I heard Captain Jeff Deptuck is coming now," the woman named Larissa said with a teasing tone. "Anything happening there? He is a fireman, after all. Perfect hero material."

"Oh, please. I'm still getting over Tyler."

The woman waved that off. "Tyler is an idiot. You and he were a waste of time."

"Besides, Jeff has his eye on Angie, another new member of the book club," Evangeline returned.

Denny smiled at the interaction. Though he didn't have a clue who they were talking about, the tone and subject of the conversation was familiar. How often had he heard his three younger sisters teasing each other about boys they liked or didn't like? For a moment he missed the three of them, wished they could be back on the home place again. Him, his three goofy sisters, his foster brother and his uncle.

He dismissed that thought as soon as it was formulated. Thanks to his ex-wife and their divorce, that time was behind all of them. He had to look to the future now. Take care of himself.

Find the peace that had eluded him ever since his parents died.

Then the woman left and Evangeline turned back to him, the smile and sparkle in her intriguing eyes disappearing as quickly as storm clouds over the sun.

Again he caught a trace of sorrow deep in her eyes, then the glitter of tears, and he felt as if, somehow, he was partly to blame.

"Hey, I'm sorry," he said.

Evangeline slipped the paper from the sale into the cash register and shoved the drawer shut. "What are you sorry for?" she muttered. "You didn't do anything."

"I dunno," he said with a shrug. "I learned from my sisters that if they're crying, it's because I did something wrong or said something wrong, so it's easier to apologize."

"I wasn't crying," she said.

Denny pushed down a sigh. Of course she wouldn't admit to it. He lifted one hand as if surrendering. "Sorry. I should know that, too."

"What do you mean?"

Denny clamped his mouth shut. When would he learn? Dealing with women was like trying to predict the weather. Just when you thought you had the direction of it, a storm would blow in and everything changed.

"So your dad told me you knew everything about the ranch," Denny said, trying to return to a more practical discussion. "That you could show me around."

Evangeline nodded, blinking quickly. She looked as though she was going to cry again.

He restrained a sigh, his practical nature warring with the big brother in him that hated seeing his sisters sad. The part that always made him feel as though he had to fix things.

"You're not okay, are you?" he asked, resting his hand beside hers on the counter. "You look kinda pale."

Evangeline snatched her hand back, tucking it under her arm as if the casual contact bothered her.

"I'm fine. Just fine," she said through lips that had grown tight and hard. "Did you want to see the apartment now?"

Denny's frown deepened. She didn't seem fine. "You sure? I can come another time if—"

"You're here now," she said. "May as well see where you'll be living for now."

Okay. Obviously he had overstepped the invisible boundary. "Sure. Of course."

Lesson learned.

She opened the old-fashioned cash register again and pulled out a key. She walked around the long wooden counter and wove her way through the stacks of shelves. Denny followed; still amazed that one place could hold so many books, surprised that people would want to buy them.

At the back of the store she opened a door that led to a hallway separating the bookstore from the apartment behind it. She crossed the hall and unlocked another heavy wooden door.

She stood aside as he walked into the room. A couple of worn leather recliners flanked the fireplace. To his right, shelves, also filled with books, lined one wall. He guessed the doors on either side of the shelves led to bedrooms.

A couch directly in front of him faced the recliners, and to his left he saw a small kitchen and another door leading to, he suspected, a bathroom.

"Looks cozy," he said, releasing a sigh of satisfaction. Though he knew he would only stay here until he could move onto the ranch, it would be perfect for now. Just enough room for him.

"The fireplace doesn't work," Evangeline said. "My grandfather put it in when he renovated this place but my dad never hooked it up."

"Grandfather?"

"My mother's father. He was the one who

owned the store. He set up the apartment upstairs where I live. My mother inherited it from him and my father from her when she…when she died." Her voice faltered.

"And you got it from your dad?" Denny asked.

Evangeline shook her head. "He still owns it."

"And the ranch?"

"Belongs to my father, as well. He inherited it from his parents."

Just as he had when his parents had died, Denny thought. Only Denny had been nineteen, too young to run a ranch on his own. Thankfully his uncle had stayed on to help him take care of the ranch and his three sisters and foster brother. It was tough, but they'd managed.

And then Lila came into the picture.…

"It's summertime," he said, turning his thoughts to the future and his plans. "I doubt I'll need a fireplace." He flashed her a grin, hoping to ease some of the tension he sensed in her.

"There're two bedrooms off the living room," she said, indicating with a lift of her chin the doors by the shelves. "One has a queen-size bed, the other a single."

Denny didn't care about the rooms, but he didn't want to appear rude, so he followed her, stopping in the doorway. The room looked like any other bedroom. Bed. Closets. Windows with flowered curtains that matched the flowered bed covering Evangeline fussed with.

"Looks nice." Then he noticed a couple of framed pictures hanging on the wall above the bed.

"Is that you and your dad?"

Evangeline glanced in the direction he pointed and nodded. "Yes, it was taken at the ranch."

She brushed her skirt as she walked past him and out the door. Her high heel caught in the carpet and she lost her balance for a moment. Denny reached out to catch her.

Her hair swung over her face as she regained her footing, releasing a whiff of her perfume.

She smelled like flowers, he thought. Delicate and feminine.

Then she pulled away.

Man, she was jumpy, he thought.

"Did you need to see the kitchen?" she asked as she walked past the couch, stopping on the other side of it, as if giving herself some distance from him. "It isn't large, but it's adequate. The stove is fiddly and the refrigerator tends to freeze vegetables if you're not careful, but it worked for my dad."

"I think I can figure it out," Denny said, content with the setup. He'd been living in motels and sharing rooms with his workers the past couple of years. He missed having a home. "When can I move in?"

"Today if you want."

"Sounds good. So my next question is when can I go out to the ranch to check it out?"

"We may as well get that out of the way. How about tomorrow morning?"

"Sunday?"

"Yeah. Is that a problem?"

"Well, I was hoping to find a church. To worship on Sunday morning."

She gave him an odd look that he wasn't sure how to interpret. Did she have a problem with him going to church?

"There's one across from Canadian Tire. It's a good church."

"Do you go?"

She shook her head. "No."

"I thought your dad said you did?" he blurted. Denny was surprised. Andy had often talked about Evangeline's strong faith.

"Not the only thing my dad seems to have wrong," she returned.

Better to leave that comment alone. "What time does church start?" he asked, changing the subject to a safer topic.

"Ten."

"Okay, how about I meet you at the ranch

after that, say one? Unless the preacher likes to go long."

"I'll see you then."

"Okay." He dragged in a long breath as one thing after another fell into place.

This was really happening. Sure, it wasn't a commitment, but it was a step in the right direction. And if leasing the ranch worked out for him, who knew...

He caught himself.

Don't plan ahead. One day at a time.

He'd learned that lesson the hard way.

"I'm guessing there's another way out of the apartment that doesn't take me through the bookstore. One that I could use to move my stuff in?"

"The hallway makes a turn and goes along the store and leads to the street," Evangeline said. "And there's another door that leads to the back parking lot. You can use that to move in."

"That's perfect. Just perfect." He glanced her way, surprised to see her looking at him.

For a moment their gazes held and once again Denny caught a flicker of sadness. Something that he suspected had to do with Andy. He still felt bad that he had been the one to deliver a message that bothered her so much. He felt a need to make it right. "And I'm sorry about...your dad, I guess. That he's not coming."

He added a quick smile and then, to his dismay, saw her lip quiver.

Oops.

She held her hand up as if to keep him at arm's length. "It's fine. I should have known better."

Known better about what?

But he didn't have the chance to ask.

"If you don't need anything else, I should get back to my store." Evangeline gave him the key then strode out the door, her skirt swaying and her long hair bouncing with every movement.

And that was Evangeline.

He just hoped he wouldn't have to do much business with her. She seemed emotional and complicated.

He had enough of that in his life.

Denny walked down the hallway, out the door and into the afternoon sunshine, stopping on the sidewalk to look at the mountains cradling the town.

For a moment he imagined what it would be like to live here. To have a home again. Build up a cow herd again.

Did he dare? Twice in his life he had lost everything. Could he risk it again?

His phone buzzed in his pocket. He was tempted to ignore it. Carlos, one of his drivers, was finishing up a haul in Prince George with one of Denny's trucks and had been calling him all morning, wondering when to bring the truck down to Hartley Creek. Denny had left a message and sent him a text. Surely that should be enough?

But habit and the reality of running his own business made him look at the phone.

And his heart thudded heavily against his ribs.

It was a text message. From Deb, his ex-wife's sister. Since his divorce from Lila two years ago, he'd never heard from her or any of Lila's family. Now Deb was texting?

Need to C U, her message said. Important. U in P G?

Why did she want to know?

Not Prince George anymore, he sent back. Hartley Creek right now. Staying awhile.

He waited a moment, then his phone tinged again.

Where living in H C? was her immediate reply.

Behind Shelf Indulgence bookstore on Main Street, he typed, wondering why she wanted to know.

He paused before sending the message, but then shrugged. Maybe Lila had something she needed to pass on just the way Andy had needed to pass something on to Evangeline.

So he shrugged, hit Send then waited. The message was delivered, but a couple of minutes later she still hadn't replied.

So what was that about?

He knew Deb had never liked him much when he and Lila were together.

Denny had been living a wild life when he'd met Lila. Every weekend, after taking care of cows and horses and family, he'd head to town to blow off steam. He'd partied too hard, met up with Lila and they'd hung out together.

One day Lila had given him the news that she was pregnant. So Denny had done the right thing and married her. Only, once that happened, Denny had found out there was no baby. Lila had figured she'd read the test wrong. She hadn't been pregnant, after all.

Denny had tried to stay true to the promises he'd made. He'd cleaned up his act. Settled down. Hung on, determined to do right by Lila.

Then, five years after they were married, Lila had decided she didn't want to hang on anymore. To satisfy the terms of the divorce, Denny had had to sell the family ranch where his sisters and foster brother still lived.

The family scattered after the ranch was sold. Denny had taken what little he'd had left after helping out his sisters and Nate, and started trucking. It was a good business. He'd taken some risks that had paid off well. Now he had a decent fleet of trucks. Of course that came with debt, but with his five-year plan he could pay that

off and afford a down payment on a new place.
A new life.

A place he would be by himself. Alone.

Just the way life worked best for him.

Chapter Two

"So what kind of deal did you and my father strike?" Evangeline asked as she and Denny walked past the corrals back to where her car and his truck were parked. A breeze teased her wavy hair around her face, flirted with the flowing skirt of her gauzy gold-and-white dress, which was loose on the top, belted at the waist.

She knew her outfit was hardly the type to go traipsing around a ranch in, but she had come directly from a meeting in Cranbrook with a toy distributor and hadn't had time to change.

Denny had obviously gone to church. He wore dark jeans, a white shirt and a corduroy blazer. He had shaved and his hair was tamed. When she'd seen him get out of his truck, she'd felt a jolt of awareness.

He cleaned up good.

"Five-year lease agreement," Denny replied.

"So it's temporary. A hobby?"

"Running yearlings is hardly a hobby," he said, sounding testy.

Evangeline shot him a surprised look. "Sorry. I understand yearlings don't require a steady time commitment."

Her father had run yearlings just before he'd leased out the ranch to other ranchers. He would buy them in the spring, run them on pasture to fatten them up, then ship them out in the fall. "Easy-peasy," he would always say. Paying hobby with no commitment.

"It's the best way for me to run my trucking business and the ranch at the same time," Denny replied.

"So no permanent plans?" No sooner had the question left her lips than she regretted asking it. It was none of her business what Denny did.

"Not yet," he said with a shrug. "I've got my gravel business going and I'm trying to set up my stake first."

No wonder he was friends with her father, Evangeline thought. Andy Arsenau always talked the same way.

"We're moving back to the ranch once I get my stake, once I have enough laid by to help us live in style," he would say. *"I want it to be perfect for you, poppet."*

She used to cling to those words whenever her

father came back to Hartley Creek throwing out promises as lightly as he threw out the cash he spent on her.

And she always believed him. Never questioned why they needed a stake to move back onto a place they'd lived before her mother died.

She pushed the depressing thoughts aside. This morning she had tried to call him again, and again she'd left a message.

She was about to ask Denny another question when his cell phone sent out a tinny whistle.

Denny looked at the screen with a crooked smile, then dropped it back into his pocket.

"Do you need to get that?" Evangeline asked.

"No. Just a text from one of my sisters. She's trekking in Nepal right now."

"That sounds interesting."

"Not the way Adrianna travels. Open ticket and plans made on the fly. No thanks," he said.

His talk of a sister created a gentle yearning. As an only child Evangeline had spent hours on her own. When she'd stayed with her aunt upstairs at the bookstore, she would create imaginary playmates. Always a sister who would play dolls or cutouts or pretend plays about princesses being rescued.

"Do you have other family besides your sisters?" she asked, suddenly curious about him.

"Yeah. Besides the three girls, a foster brother."

"Do they live close by?"

Denny shook his head. "Adrianna lives wherever she is working. Olivia and Trista are tree planting up in northern B.C. this summer. And Nate..." Denny's voice trailed off and he gave a shrug. "Last I heard, he was at a cutting horse competition in Elko."

"That's a lot of family," she said with a wistful note in her voice. "And your parents?"

"They died in a plane crash when I was nineteen."

A shadow crossed his face and Evangeline saw that the memory still caused him pain. In that moment Evangeline felt a bond between them. A bond between children whose parents had left a family too soon.

At least she still had her father.

"I'm sorry to hear that," she said, sympathy softening her voice. "That must have been so difficult."

"We got through it. I'm sure you know how that works. You lost your mother, too."

Then he gave her a rueful smile, which, combined, with his acknowledgment of her own pain and history, made her heart flutter. Just a bit.

She returned his smile and as their eyes held, awareness bloomed.

Evangeline caught herself and looked away. This was not the man for her.

"Besides the house, is there anything else you need to know about the place?" Evangeline asked, feeling a sudden need to get this tour over and done with. From the first moment she'd met Denny, she'd felt as if her emotions were a tangle that she couldn't sort out.

She'd thought Tyler was the right man, and look how that had turned out. Andy Arsenau had broken Evangeline's heart enough times that she would be crazy to feel anything for someone exactly like him. She didn't trust her judgment in men anymore. "I'm sure my father filled you in," she continued.

"I think I've seen what I need to see," he said, giving her another crooked grin.

"Okay, then," she said, then turned and walked toward her car, signaling the end of the tour.

They arrived at the vehicles but Evangeline stopped there, drumming her fingers on the hood of her car. "How did you meet my father? How did you know about the ranch?" she blurted, unable to contain her curiosity about Denny and Andy.

Denny scratched his forehead with a fingertip as if wondering himself.

"We met at a truck stop. We were on the same gravel haul. I'd seen him a couple of times before, and we ended up sitting together. Talking. That was about a year ago. We clicked. We started arranging to meet when our schedules worked. One day he told me he had this place that wasn't getting used to its potential. I told him I was looking for a place for a few years and he offered to lease me this ranch. He talked about you a lot and said he missed you—"

"So what kind of truck do you drive?" she cut in, her disappointment with her father too fresh to hear false platitudes.

Denny's frown made her regret her sharp tone, but at the same time she wasn't in the mood to hear secondhand about her father's affection for her.

"I have three gravel trucks," he said. "They keep me busy."

Of course they did. The more she talked to Denny, the more she understood how her father would have connected with this guy. They had so much in common.

"Then if you've seen what you need, I guess we're done here," she said, pulling her keys out of her purse. If she stood here long enough she would get angry with her father again and that was an exercise in futility. She had to move on from the past.

But as she drove away, she glanced in her rearview mirror at the man who stood by his truck looking over the ranch with the same expression she had caught on his face as they'd walked the yard.

As though it was home. A place he belonged.

Evangeline tore her attention away, memories, long buried, assaulting her.

She and her mother working in the garden....

Riding in the hills with her father and mother to check the cattle on the upper pasture....

Coming home from the bookstore after spending Saturdays there with her mother, carrying crinkly bags filled with new books and heading directly to her favorite spot in the shade of a large fir tree where she could see both the ranch yard and the mountains guarding it....

It had been the best time in her life. A time when she'd felt safe. Protected. Loved. Life was perfect.

Then her mother had died.

She and her father had stayed on the ranch for a month before she'd moved in with Auntie Josie at age eight.

From that time until she was nineteen, Evangeline had spent her spare time in the store helping her aunt manage it for her father. When her aunt decided she wanted to live closer to her sister, she'd moved away, leaving Evangeline in charge for the past nine years.

Her father had promised she would get the store

when she turned twenty-one. She was twenty-eight now and still no closer to full ownership.

Her throat thickened as she turned onto the road. Why did her father's broken promises still bother her?

I'm not going to cry, she told herself, reminding herself of other disappointments as she clamped her hands on the steering wheel. *I'm a big girl. I shouldn't care about another broken promise.*

I'm not going to cry.

And then she did precisely that.

Was that crying he heard?

Denny wove his shirt onto the metal hanger, dropped it onto the bar in the cupboard, then paused, listening.

But whatever he'd heard had stopped.

Must have imagined it, he thought, picking up another shirt. After touring the ranch with Evangeline Sunday, he had spent yesterday moving the few things he owned into the apartment. He had to finish today. Tomorrow he had to arrange to get the trucks moved and Friday he'd start work.

His yearlings were coming to the ranch in a couple of weeks. Which gave him time to do the work necessary to get the ranch ready.

He hooked the hanger on the bar in the closet,

trying not to let his thoughts crowd in on him. Too much to do and too little time.

He paused.

There was that baby crying again. This was followed by the murmur of a woman's voice. The crying grew louder, then stopped.

Then he heard someone pounding on his door.

He stepped around the last couple of boxes he had to unpack and opened the wooden door of his apartment.

A tall, thin woman with lanky brown hair stood in the hallway with her back to him. She wore blue jeans and a discolored purple hoodie. A black bag was hooked over one arm; a suitcase lay at her feet.

She was holding a little girl, who looked to be a year and a half old, wearing a stained, white sleeper. The toddler had sandy, curly hair, brown eyes shimmering with tears and a mustache of orange juice. She stared at him over the woman's shoulder, her lip quivering.

"Can I help you?" Denny asked.

The woman turned and Denny's heart fell like a stone as he recognized Deb.

His sister-in-law. Ex-sister-in-law, he corrected.

"Hey, Denny. Long time no see," she said in her raspy, smoker's voice. She jiggled the baby a moment, then held her up, handing her to Denny.

"Hang on to her a minute, wouldja?"

Not sure what else to do, Denny took the little girl, catching a whiff of cigarette smoke and old milk.

"What is going on?" he asked just as the toddler pushed at him with sticky hands, whimpering again.

Deb handed him the black diaper bag, then pushed the suitcase toward him with her sneakered foot. "You may as well know, and I don't know how to tell you better than this, but Lila's dead."

Denny stared at her, his grip loosening on the baby in his shocked surprise.

The little girl whimpered and he quickly pulled her close again, trying to wrap his head around what Deb had so causally thrown at him.

Lila? Dead? Why hadn't anyone told him?

"What? When?" The questions tumbled out of his shocked confusion. "How did it happen?"

"She got sick about three months ago," Deb said, crossing her thin arms over her chest, looking down at the floor as if still remembering. "Got some infection from a cut. Never got better. She died in the hospital a month ago."

All this was delivered in an emotionless monotone that beat at him like waves on sand.

Denny's heart slowed and then sped up as reality slowly sunk in.

"A month? You never thought I should know

this?" Denny felt a white-hot anger mingled with sorrow growing in his gut as his brain caught up with the information Deb had thrown at him so casually.

The baby let out another whimper and he realized he'd been holding her too tight. He eased off, anger still coursing through him.

"You were divorced," Deb said, as if that explained everything. "Didn't think you would care. Lila always said you two fought like cats and dogs. Besides, I didn't have your number and Lila's phone got stolen in the hospital. Took me this long to track you down." Her voice grew shriller with each word and Denny struggled to stifle his own anger with her, reminding himself that Deb had also recently lost her sister.

But at least she'd had a month to deal with it.

As her words found a place in his mind, awareness of the weight and warmth of the sticky little girl he held worked its way through his fog of confusion.

"And who is this?" he asked, dropping the diaper bag Deb had handed him into the hallway and looking down at the little girl.

She stared up at him, her deep brown eyes unblinking. Cute little thing even if she looked and smelled as though she needed a bath.

Deb only looked past him into the apartment,

nodding as if she approved, then looked back at the little girl now tucked against Denny's hip.

"That's Ella. Your daughter."

"What?" The word burst out of him as another shock jolted him. "No. That's impossible." Denny glanced at the little girl he was holding. His angry outburst had erased the smile and her lip quivered again.

He jiggled her to settle her down as he looked back at Deb.

"No way."

"Yes, way." Deb continued, "Lila found out she was pregnant after you guys signed the final divorce papers."

"She was lying. She's done this before." Denny felt like he was on an amusement park ride, his head going one way, his body another, and nothing making any sense. Even in his shock he thought of the fake pregnancy that had gotten them married.

"She wasn't seeing anyone before or after she divorced you. Your name is on the birth certificate as the dad."

As Deb spoke it was as if her words barreled toward him from the far end of a tunnel. He stared at her as his mind slipped back to his last months with Lila. She had been miserable, staying away all hours, never coming home, and when she was home, all she did was yell at him and complain about being on the ranch.

Denny had started going back to church, trying to find the strength to keep their relationship going. One night she had come home early, in tears. He had asked her if she was unhappy because she was seeing someone else, but she had vehemently denied that.

So he'd convinced her to try again. She had agreed, and he'd believed her. After months of being apart, they had been intimate.

The next day she'd left and the next week he'd been served with divorce papers.

When he'd called her to find out why, she had said it was because she wasn't happy on the ranch. Never would be and it wasn't fair to him to stick around and prolong the agony. Those motives had started to sound pretty suspect when Denny found out how much money she'd wanted to settle the divorce.

Denny looked back at the little girl. The girl Deb said was his daughter. "How old is she?"

"Eighteen months."

"She can't be mine," he protested, unwilling to believe what Deb was saying.

"The certificate is in the diaper bag if you want to check," Deb was saying. "And so is her health care card. You'll need that if she gets sick."

"Why didn't Lila tell me about her?" he insisted as the baby squirmed. "She never said anything about this pregnancy."

"She said you two never talked after you split."

That much was true. Lila's petition for divorce had been a shock, but at the same time a small relief. In spite of his last-ditch effort to keep the marriage going, when he'd received the papers he'd decided not to contest it. Nor had he had any desire to be in contact with her.

The proceedings had been a financial drain. Once Denny had walked away from Lila with precious little in the bank and a bitter taste in his mouth after having to sell the family ranch, he couldn't face her again. Apparently the feeling had been mutual. He'd never heard from her over the past two years.

"I told her to tell you but she said something about how you wouldn't believe her. But I pushed and she promised me she would. Obviously she didn't." Deb shot a pointed look at the little girl in his arms.

"Anyhow, when she got sick I took care of Ella, but I got another job and another boyfriend and can't take care of the munchkin anymore. You know me. Not crazy about kids. Then I figured, hey, she's your kid. You should be the one to do it. Took me a bit to track you down, and so here you are. Clothes are in the suitcase, diapers in the bag. She drinks out of a sippy cup and doesn't like strawberries. There's more info on a paper in the suitcase."

Denny's brain spun a few more times as he tried to regain his balance. Tried to regain control of the situation.

"What about your parents? Do they know about this?"

"Of course they do. But they told me that I had to do the right thing and find you. Besides, after Lila died, they left on some project out in Bolivia. Can't get hold of them until they call me. And they won't be back for about a month or so. So here I am."

The information she threw at him was like a landslide. One thing after another, leaving him feeling buried.

"How did you find me?" was all he got out as the little girl wriggled in his arms.

"My boyfriend's friend did some carpentry work for a guy who drove a truck. We met him at a bar. Found out the guy used to work for you. He gave us your number."

Might have been Stewart, a driver he had fired a couple months back. Probably had it in for him, Denny thought. Awesome.

Then the little girl whimpered and he jiggled her, still not sure what he was supposed to do, trying to find a way to reason with Lila's sister. Trying to wrap his head around Lila's death.

Then Deb took a step back and waggled her fingers at the child. "Be good for Daddy, Ella," she said. Then, without another word, she turned and strode down the hallway and around the corner.

What? She was leaving the baby behind?

Denny looked from the now-empty hallway to the howling little girl, trying to figure out which emotion to hang on to. Fear. Anger. Confusion.

Concern for the little girl in his arms.

"Deb," he called out, "come back here. We need to talk about this. This can't be my baby."

But the only thing he heard was the echo of Ella's pathetic cries.

Of course his phone would chime right then. He yanked it out of his pocket as if hoping to find some answers there. But it was just his sister Olivia. Asking him to send her money again.

He'd deal with that later.

Then the door to the bookstore opened and there stood Evangeline, her shining hair flowing in waves over her shoulders, her white dress giving her an ethereal look.

And she was looking at him as if he was crazy.

"Everything okay?" she asked, though clearly she could see it wasn't. He was holding a crying baby and yelling at an empty hallway.

Denny looked from Evangeline to Ella and felt his heart sink.

What was he supposed to do with a baby?

Chapter Three

"Do you need a hand?" Evangeline asked, the howls of the little girl catching at her heart.

She had heard a commotion in the hallway and, curious, had stepped out just in time to hear a baby crying. Then she saw the little girl in Denny's arms and heard him calling out to someone named Deb.

The baby was screaming now, batting at Denny with her hands.

Denny looked as if someone had punched him in the stomach. He leaned against the doorjamb like a sailor on a storm-tossed boat clinging to a mast.

Pity rushed through her at his confusion.

"Yeah. No." He grabbed his head with his free hand, tousled his long, thick hair, then shook his head.

The child's howls were piercing. She flailed,

arching her back, looking wildly around as if seeking a familiar face. Denny patted her back with one huge hand, looking completely at a loss.

Big, fat tears spilled down the little girl's cheeks and her sorrow caught at Evangeline's heart.

Without thinking, she took the little bundle of brokenhearted humanity out of Denny's arms and held her close.

Then she caught a whiff of something unpleasant.

"She needs a clean diaper," Evangeline said.

Denny dragged his hand over his face and looked down at the bag lying at his feet.

"Deb said something about diapers in here," he mumbled, his eyes flicking from the bag to the empty hallway as if hoping this Deb person would return.

"Give me a minute," Evangeline said, rocking the child as she walked back into her store. It was almost closing time anyway, so she locked up and turned the sign over. She'd get the lights later.

Then she walked back through the quiet store, the little girl's sobs subsiding somewhat.

"Hey, hey, it's okay," Evangeline cooed, holding her close as she walked back to the apartment. Denny was still standing in the hallway, looking as stunned as he had a few moments ago.

"Let's get her cleaned up," Evangeline said,

cutting him a quick glance. "Bring the bag to the bathroom. I'll take care of this."

Sticky hands clung to her and Evangeline's heart stuttered as she held the little girl close. Poor little person, she thought, clearly remembering the times she'd gotten dumped, in this very building, on her aunt's doorstep upstairs when her father decided it was time to go.

She had been a lot older but often just as upset.

"It's okay. It's okay," she murmured, rocking the baby as her sobs slowly subsided into hiccups. Then, when she took in a last, shuddering cry, Evangeline gently pulled back, her hand on the little girl's shoulder.

Chocolate-brown eyes, the same color as Denny's, stared back at her, tears still sparkling on eyelashes as long and thick as Denny's.

"This can't be my baby," she had heard him yell. But in spite of his protest the little girl bore a striking resemblance to him.

"Here's the bag," Denny said from behind her.

Evangeline nodded, gently laying the baby on the counter. "How old is she?"

"I think she's eighteen months."

"You're not sure how old your baby is?"

Denny lifted one hand in a helpless gesture. "I knew nothing about her till now."

"And her name?" she said, keeping focused on what was at hand.

"Ella." Denny heaved out a sigh, leaning against the doorjamb, watching as Evangeline unzipped the stained sleeper.

"Does she have any other clothes?" Evangeline asked, making a face at the sight of the equally stained onesie underneath the sleeper.

"Deb said there was some in the suitcase," Denny muttered. By the time he returned, Evangeline had filled the tub with water and had dealt with the dirty diaper. The sleeper and onesie she had tossed into a pile.

Ella was quiet now, her unblinking eyes flickering from Denny to Evangeline. Back and forth, back and forth, as if trying to figure out what she was supposed to do with these two strangers.

Evangeline looked around for soap and was surprised to find a bar already set out.

"Do you have a clean towel?" she asked.

"Yeah. Um. I'll get it." He pulled open a cupboard door and Ella turned her wide eyes to Evangeline as if seeking answers to questions she couldn't articulate.

"Hey, little one," Evangeline said, cupping the warm water and pouring it over her body. She shot a glance over her shoulder at Denny, who hovered in the background, his hands shoved into the pockets of his blue jeans, looking puzzled and concerned at the same time.

"So why do you think she's not your daughter?"

Denny blew out a sigh. "Deb said my name is on the birth certificate. But Lila and I were married for five years and she never became pregnant. I thought she couldn't have kids. But if she's eighteen months old, as Deb says she is, maybe. She might be." He blew out another sigh as he stepped closer, as if to get a better look at his daughter.

Evangeline felt her initial reaction to Denny had been justified. No hero material here.

She finished washing Ella, who was quiet now, which made Evangeline even more concerned than her outraged sorrow had.

"Can you hand me the towel?" she asked, pulling the plug in the bathtub.

A thick yellow towel appeared over her shoulder. She wrapped it around Ella's shining little body and patted her dry.

"Do you have the bag of clothes?" she asked, turning to get up. But the weight of Ella sent her off balance and she stumbled.

Denny caught her by the arms, steadying her. His hands were large and warm and solid.

She looked up at him, surprised to see him staring down at her, a peculiar light in his eyes. Then he blinked and Evangeline wondered if she had imagined it. He released her and stepped aside.

"The suitcase with the clothes is in the living

room," he muttered as Evangeline walked past him. "I picked some out."

Ella was quiet as Evangeline set her on the floor beside the suitcase, then sat, cross-legged, to dress her.

"I don't know if the clothes are okay," Denny muttered, hovering behind her. "Wasn't much to choose from…" He let the sentence trail off, as if unsure what to say.

Evangeline choked down a laugh at the sight of the tiny blue flannel shirt and blue jeans he had laid out on the floor. Exactly like the clothes he favored.

She found another onesie and some socks among the sparse offering of clothing and made quick work of putting another diaper on Ella and then the onesie. Settling the little girl on her lap, she wrestled her feet into the socks, then the blue jeans. Then she worked the shirt onto the now-squirming little girl.

By the time Evangeline snapped up the shirt, Ella was leaning away from her. She elbowed Evangeline in her chest as she scrambled to her feet. She fell, quickly pushed herself upright, then toddled over to an empty box in the middle of the living room and started pushing it.

Her hair was a mess of damp curls. Evangeline would have to wait for Ella to settle down before running a brush through them.

"She seems happier," Denny said, dropping into a chair beside Evangeline, resting his elbows on his knees.

Evangeline pulled her knees up, wrapped her arms around them, her skirt puddling onto the floor around her legs. In contrast to her wails of a few moments ago, Ella now made no sound at all, seemingly content to push the empty box around the floor.

But happy? Evangeline doubted it. The little girl had a look of adult resignation on her face. She didn't even so much as look at either Evangeline or Denny, her entire concentration on the box.

"So now what?" Evangeline asked.

Denny heaved out a sigh and Evangeline shot a quick look his way. He was staring at Ella, her dirty onesie and sleeper dangling from his hands, still looking as confused as when she'd first walked in on them.

"I have no idea."

"This Deb woman you were yelling at..." Evangeline paused, not sure how much she was allowed to ask of someone she had only met a couple of days ago.

"My sister-in-law," he said. "Lila's sister."

"And Lila is your wife?"

"Was my wife." This elicited another sigh. "Deb just told me that she died...that she died a month ago." Denny stopped there, his voice breaking, and Evangeline reached out and laid her hand on his arm.

Denny shot her a quick look of thanks. "I didn't know she was sick. We had been divorced for a couple of years. We didn't stay in touch." He released a harsh laugh. "Deb didn't even call me when she died. I knew Deb disliked me, but really..." His voice faded away as he shook his head again.

"You didn't know about Lila's death before today?"

"Not a clue." Denny bunched the clothes in his hands, his knuckles growing white. "She was my wife and I had to hear about it like this." Denny dropped the clothes and shoved his hands through his hair.

"I'm so sorry," Evangeline murmured, not sure what else to say. She felt bad for the man. "That must be hard news."

They were quiet a moment, then Denny dragged his hand over his face, rasping on the stubble on his chin. "It is. A bit. Trouble is Lila and I weren't close. After the divorce she never wrote, never called. But she was my wife. I should have been told. I would have gone to the funeral."

Evangeline caught the plaintive note in his deep voice. It wasn't hard to see that in spite of what he said about his ex-wife, he had cared for her.

So what had happened to instigate the divorce?

She dismissed the question as quickly as it formed. She didn't need to get involved with Denny's obviously messy past.

"So what's the story with Ella, then?" she asked, watching the toddler push the box around, her passive expression more heartbreaking than her tears had been. This little child had been uprooted from her life, dropped into someone else's, with no consideration for her feelings. Who knew what she was thinking.

"I don't know. Deb shows up out of the blue with this little girl, saying she's mine," Denny said, confusion clouding his features. "If she is, why didn't I hear about this sooner?"

Evangeline wasn't sure what to say, either. Denny's life had obviously taken a complicated turn.

Trouble was, she had already spent more time than she should here. But she felt bad leaving Denny with this little girl.

She glanced at her watch. "Sorry, I should go." She had yet to make her supper. Her book club was coming tonight and she had to make coffee and prepare the room.

"Of course." He looked up at her and the look of sheer terror on his face made her smile at the sight of such a large man brought to such confusion by a toddler. "So what do I do next?"

Ella had stopped pushing her box and was staring at him as if wondering herself what was happening.

"She's probably hungry or thirsty," Evangeline suggested.

Denny shrugged. "What does someone her age eat? I haven't even had time to go grocery shopping."

He looked so confused that Evangeline felt a glimmer of sympathy for the guy. This had to be overwhelming.

She felt torn between her schedule and giving Denny some support.

You were once that little girl.

The thought wound through her mind, pulling at memories of watching her father disappear, leaving her with a woman who cared for her but didn't care about her.

"Tell you what," she said. "I'm done for the day. I can help you pick out what you might need."

She could call Emma. She had a young son and her little girl was about six months old by now. She would know what to get. Mia, next door, would have advice, as well, but Evangeline knew she was far too busy with her store and her own family.

Denny shot her such a look of gratitude that, for a moment, Evangeline felt her heart soften toward the guy.

But just for a moment.

I'm helping him because of Ella, she told herself as she walked back to the store.

It has nothing to do with him. Nothing at all.

"Deb said she's about a year and a half," Denny said, following Evangeline down the grocery store aisle. "And so does her birth certificate."

The birth certificate with his name on it.

He glanced over at Ella, still trying to absorb the reality of this little girl in his life.

Ella sat in the seat of the grocery cart, her hair a fluff of golden curls, her chubby hands clinging to the handle of the cart. She looked nothing like the happy babies smiling back at him from the variety of food jars, boxes and tins filling the shelves.

He wondered if she knew, on some level, that she had been abandoned. Poor kid.

"If she is, I'm thinking she can eat more solid food," Evangeline was saying. "At least, that's what Emma told me."

Apparently, Emma was—from the way Evangeline was quoting her as they stocked up on food, diapers, wipes, juice and snacks—the resident expert on all things baby.

Emma was also providing them with a car seat that she said she would bring to the grocery store when they were done here. Deb hadn't left him a car seat when she dropped Ella off, which made him wonder if she'd used one at all. He pushed that thought aside. He didn't want to dwell on Deb and her poor choices. For now he had to keep his focus on Ella.

Evangeline laid her choices in the buggy and continued down the aisle, the wonky wheel of the cart squeaking as they went.

As he followed, Denny couldn't help but notice the swing of her hair, the grace of her movements. She was a beautiful woman. Even prettier than the pictures Andy had showed him.

Don't go there, he reminded himself, thinking of her comments about church when he'd first met her. Being with Lila had taught him to seek someone who shared his faith. Shared his beliefs.

And on top of that, what woman would want to have anything to do with a guy whose life was such a mess?

"I never knew this part of the grocery store even existed," Denny said, eyeing the endless shelves of baby food, diapers and assorted other paraphernalia that, it seemed, Ella needed, as well.

"So what parts of the grocery store do you

shop in? Or don't you buy groceries?" Evangeline asked, slanting him a puzzled look.

"I heard a piece on the radio that said everything you need is on the outside ring of the store, so that's where I get what I need. Then a quick trip down the frozen-food aisle and, bam, done." He emphasized his comment with a fist on an open palm.

Evangeline laughed at that; a breathy sound with a little sigh at the end that caught his heart.

He blamed his reaction to it on basic loneliness and being around an attractive woman.

"And now you'll have to add this aisle to your shopping repertoire," Evangeline said, setting a box of what looked like huge tongue depressors into the cart.

Denny sighed. "At least until I figure out what to do."

"What do you mean?" Evangeline asked, consulting her list, then looking up at him.

Denny spread his hands out in a gesture of surrender. "I don't know how to take care of this little girl. Not properly. I have my business to run, the ranch to get ready." He sighed, pushed his hat back on his head and gestured at the slowly filling cart. "And now I have to figure out where to put all this stuff in the apartment."

"It does seem like a lot of food," Evangeline

agreed as she came to the end of the aisle and turned toward the dairy section.

"So what are we getting now?" Denny asked, pulling his phone out of his pocket to check for messages. There were no notifications on the screen.

Carlos was supposed to have called him to tell him how the job had gone. Denny needed to know so that he could make arrangements to move the truck here to Hartley Creek.

"Milk and yogurt and eggs." Evangeline held up a list she had compiled, glancing from it to the containers of milk lined up in the dairy case. She reached for a huge jug and dropped it into the cart, plucked a box of mini yogurts off the shelf and a carton of eggs, then, finally, folded the list and put it in her pocket. "I think we're done."

"I would think so, too," Denny said, scratching his head with his forefinger. "I can't believe one little girl like Ella needs all this stuff."

"I don't know anything about babies, so I just have to go with what Emma told me."

"You never had any younger brothers or sisters you had to take care of?"

"My father obviously never told you I was an only child." She flashed Denny a tight smile, then turned the cart around.

Once again Denny followed her down the aisle toward the cashiers.

Right. He had forgotten about that.

And she seemed touchy about it, to boot.

He wanted to tell her that having siblings was fun, but it had its responsibilities and moments of hardship. Especially when he'd had to tell his sisters and foster brother that the ranch they had grown up on had to be sold because of his bad decision.

He pushed that memory aside. That was then. This was now. Only, now also included one last souvenir of Lila.

A little girl he'd never known existed until today.

Evangeline laid the stuff on the conveyor belt and chatted up the cashier as she rang the groceries through the till. A young couple waved hello as they walked past, and an older woman stopped to ask her a question about book club.

Denny felt a hint of melancholy as he watched Evangeline's interactions. At one time he, too, had been part of a community. Had been able to go to town and talk with most anyone.

Now he was running around from job to job, trying to scrabble together enough money to someday settle down again.

He glanced over at Ella, who stared at him with solemn eyes.

He gave her a tentative smile, wondering how

in the world he was supposed to untangle this particular knot in his life. Why hadn't Lila told him?

Would you have believed her?

Probably not.

"We're done here," Evangeline said, looking over at Denny as the cashier bagged the groceries.

"Right. Sorry." He pulled his wallet out and handed a couple of bills to the cashier.

As the cashier gave him the change, Evangeline's phone beeped. She yanked it out of her purse but then, as she glanced at the screen, she seemed to deflate as if she'd hoped the caller would be someone else.

Andy maybe?

"Emma is waiting for us in the parking lot," she said.

Denny shoved the change into his pocket and once again followed Evangeline out the door.

When they got near to where Denny's truck was parked, a woman stepped out of a pickup beside his, waving at them.

"Hey, Evangeline. Over here."

Emma, Denny presumed. She had long brown hair, dark brown eyes and an infectious grin. Her blue jeans had grass stains on the knees and her white T-shirt had streaks of dirt. Evangeline had mentioned she lived on a ranch, and she obviously did more than just keep house.

"Hey, Emma, great timing," Evangeline said, pushing the cart toward the truck.

As Evangeline parked the cart, Emma walked around to the other side of her truck. She opened the door and wrestled out a large seat. As she pulled it, a strap got caught and she almost dropped it.

Denny hurried over to help her, earning him a bright smile. "Thanks. I'm guessing you're Daddy?" Emma asked.

Denny felt a flush warm his neck as he took the car seat from her. "Apparently."

Emma's puzzled look bounced from him to Evangeline, looking for more information.

"Emma, can you help Denny put the seat in the back of the car?" was all Evangeline said.

Denny heaved the surprisingly heavy seat into his truck and strapped it down. As he buckled Ella into it, he thought back to when he and Lila were married.

A good friend of his, Lance, had stopped by with his boy. Denny remembered watching Lance buckle the little boy into the car seat parked in the backseat of his friend's candy-apple-red truck. This was a vehicle Lance had spent hours waxing, polishing and babying. A truck Denny wished he had.

But crumbs from crackers and leftover papers from fast-food meals had littered the backseat of

Lance's pride and joy, and Lance hadn't seemed to care. His little boy was his pride and joy.

And once again Denny had been envious.

Now he had his own fancy truck that he had scrimped and scraped to purchase. And now it had a car seat in it, as well.

But somehow it wasn't the same situation.

He straightened, looking at Ella, who was staring back at him, her dark eyes so serious. Her expression so solemn.

"She's a quiet one," Emma said with a laugh.

"Yeah. She is." It didn't seem natural. He remembered his sisters at this age, laughing and squirming and getting into all kinds of mischief.

He closed the back door on Ella, then helped Evangeline load the last of the groceries into the other side of the truck.

When they were done he turned back to Emma, who stood by her own truck, her arms folded across her T-shirt.

"Thanks so much for the use of the car seat," Denny said.

"Gotta keep the little munchkin safe," Emma returned.

"Yeah. That I do."

He pulled his car keys out of his pocket and opened the door for Evangeline.

She gave him a curious look, then stepped up

into the truck, tucking her long, flowing skirt underneath her as he shut the door.

Emma was watching him, a bemused light in her eyes. "I heard you're leasing Andy's place," she said. "My husband, Carter, and I run a ranch up Morrisey Creek. If you ever need help, we're willing to lend a hand."

"Thanks. That's good to know." Denny blew out a sigh, thinking about the work that lay ahead of him. "I might take you up on that offer."

"Make sure you do." Emma gave him a quick wave, then got into her truck and drove away.

As Denny sat behind the wheel of his truck he glanced at Ella again, who stared back at him.

"Is that normal?" he asked Evangeline as he started up his truck, worry digging at him. "She cried like crazy when she first came, but hasn't given a peep since."

Evangeline looked back at Ella, her own concern showing. "She's probably confused and afraid. She doesn't know who you are, so she's going to be cautious."

Denny shook his head as he pulled out of the parking lot. "I just wish I knew what I'm supposed to do. I've got a hundred things on my plate."

"I'd start with feeding her."

Denny nodded. Of course. That made sense. "And after that?"

"Bedtime."

"And tomorrow?"

"Just do what comes next," Evangeline returned. "That's how I got through it all."

Denny shot her a puzzled glance. He wanted to ask her what she meant by her cryptic comment, but when he saw her pursed lips and tight expression, he guessed she wasn't sharing.

And why should she? She was as much of a stranger to him as he was to Ella.

His mind ticked back to Ella's mother and his heart floundered.

Lila. Why hadn't anyone told him?

Dear Lord, he prayed, *give me strength to get through this. Help me do what Evangeline said. Help me to trust in You to figure out what comes next.*

And what was next? Try to get hold of Lila's parents somehow? Find someone else to take care of Ella? Get his trucking business moved?

Do what comes next? If only it was that easy.

Or that painless.

Chapter Four

"This book was too depressing." Mia Verbeek tilted her head to one side, her dark eyes, emphasized by the pixie cut she favored, flashing as if challenging anyone else gathered in the back room of Shelf Indulgence to dispute her opinion. "I would not have read it if it wasn't a book club book. After taking care of four kids all day, reading about this woman's struggle to love was a downer."

"I found it challenged my view of the romance of family life," Angie, one of the newer members of the book club, said, slipping her green-rimmed glasses back on her face.

"I'm voting for depressing," Jeff Deptuck said, leaning forward, his grin encompassing the entire group. With his light brown hair, high cheekbones and the faint cleft in his stubbled chin, he exuded charm and goodwill.

"Of course you would, Captain Sunny-Side-Up Deptuck," Angie returned.

Evangeline held back a grin, watching the sparring between Jeff and Angie, the latest additions to the Hartley Creek book club that met at the bookstore.

Everyone in the book club knew that Jeff had a not-so-secret crush on Angie. Trouble was, Angie was very vocal about her resistance to any form of romance.

"I still say it was worth a read," Renee Albertson replied, twirling a strand of her brown hair around her finger, closing the book on her lap and looking around at the other members. "It wasn't as over the top as the police procedural Mia insisted we read last time."

"I have to agree with Mia's take on the book," Sophie Brouwer spoke up, her blue eyes twinkling, her permed white hair bobbing as she nodded. "This book was dark and sad. I'm surprised you chose a story like this, Renee, given that your own life is in such a happy place right now."

Renee just smiled as Evangeline stifled a flare of envy.

Renee's fiancé, Zach, was the perfect hero. Kind. Considerate. Attractive in a cultured sort of way.

Just the kind of guy she would have loved to find and still hoped that she would. Someday.

A thump from the other side of the hallway caught everyone's attention and made Evangeline sit up.

When she and Denny had returned from the grocery store, she'd seen he was at a loss for what to do. So she'd helped him feed Ella and get her sleeper and diaper on for the evening. While she'd given Ella a bottle, he'd set up the portable crib they'd bought at the hardware store. When she'd finally left, Ella was sleeping. Even so, she'd felt as if she was abandoning him, but she'd had her own schedule to keep.

And while she felt bad for Denny, he was a virtual stranger to her and on some level she wanted to keep some distance between them.

"Is that your new neighbor?" Mia asked, her eyes flashing with anticipation.

Evangeline clutched her book, her eyes riveted on the pages she had opened it to. She didn't want to think about Denny moving into her father's space across the hall. Two weeks ago she had told this same group, with much anticipation, how her father was coming back and soon this store would be hers.

Time to cash that reality check.

"He's probably rearranging the furniture to make room for Ella's crib," she said, flipping a page of the book and looking up, ready to change the subject. "I found it interesting that it took the heroine half of the book to realize what she wanted."

"I still can't believe someone dumped a baby on him," Angie said, obviously not ready to drop the topic of Denny. "Who would do that?"

"You don't always know what a person is going through or why they make the decisions they do," Renee said quietly, giving Angie a careful smile that spoke of tough choices Renee herself had made in her own life.

"That was kind of you to help him out with that little girl," Sophie Brouwer said, patting Evangeline on her arm.

"I couldn't leave him alone to figure it out." Though she still felt bad for leaving him when she had. Trouble was, how much could she realistically do? She barely knew Denny as it was.

"Poor guy probably didn't have a clue," Mia said. "I have to say I'm crushed that you didn't call to ask for my advice."

"You're way too busy with your shop and your four kids," Evangeline returned.

"That's the truth," Mia said with a sigh. "I'm just thankful I could get Blythe to watch the kids tonight."

"So what's the deal with this Denny guy?" Renee queried. "I thought you said he was leasing the ranch?"

"Apparently he's trucking and ranching. Just

like my dad." Evangeline couldn't keep the faintly bitter note out of her voice. Her own feelings about her father were still a confusion of anger and disappointment. But simmering beneath this was a frustration that he still created this storm of mixed emotions. She'd thought, after all these years, she had insulated her heart from her father's unmet expectations.

And he still hadn't called her.

"What's he like?" Mia asked, leaning forward in her chair. "Hero material?"

"He's a trucker and a cowboy. Neither of which are my type, so have at 'im, girl," Evangeline said with a dismissive wave of her hand.

"I've got a divorce behind me and four kids to raise. Not interested," Mia said with a short laugh. "Though Kelly at Mug Shots says he's got that rugged good-looking thing going," Mia continued, as if trying to persuade her friend to give the guy a chance. "And apparently he has gorgeous eyes."

"Why are you rhapsodizing over him if you're not interested?"

"I was thinking of you. You're always looking for a hero."

"I'm a hero," Jeff put in with a wink.

Evangeline laughed. "You're a fireman. You're everybody's hero."

"Only to some," he said, cutting a quick glance Angie's way.

But Angie was looking at her book, her long blond hair falling across her face, the corner of her lip tucked between her teeth.

The way Jeff looked at Angie created a twitch of envy. *She doesn't know what she's missing,* Evangeline thought.

"You're looking pensive," Emma spoke up, giving her a secret smile as if she knew what Evangeline was thinking. "Something bugging you?"

Evangeline gave her a tight smile followed by a light shake of her head. Evangeline and Emma had become good friends when Emma had moved to Hartley Creek a few years ago. Evangeline had stood up for Emma when she'd married Carter. Tyler had been her escort to the wedding.

Evangeline remembered too well how she'd felt at that wedding, dancing with Tyler. His attentiveness and good looks were the epitome of everything Evangeline had hoped for in a future husband. In fact he had made Evangeline hope that someday she might be escorted down the aisle wearing a white dress and translucent veil.

But she'd discovered Tyler liked the idea of a girlfriend more than the idea of a wife. And from the way her father was acting she doubted she could count on him to be present should that momentous day ever come.

Evangeline caught herself and gave herself a mental face palm. *Enough with the gloomy thoughts. Move on. Follow your own advice to Denny. Do what comes next.*

Another thump from across the hall caught her attention. Seriously, what was he doing over there? Obviously moving in was noisy work.

"So now we need to decide on a book for next time," Sophie Brouwer was saying. "Any suggestions? Evangeline, you usually have some good ideas."

Evangeline glanced down at the list of books she had, indeed, come to book club with. But as she looked at the titles she released a wry smile. One was about a young girl being reconciled with a father after a long separation during the California Gold Rush. The other was about a father looking for his lost daughter during the Spanish Civil War.

Definitely a theme going on here.

"I don't think any of these would work." She folded the paper and tucked it into the pocket of her sweater, ignoring Mia's puzzled look.

"How about *Arctic Grail?*" Jeff suggested.

Mia shivered. "Brr. Sounds like a winter book again. I hereby declare no books about winter in summer. In fact no books about winter even in winter. We get enough winter in Hartley Creek."

"I have some ideas," Eloise Beck said.

She gave her recommendations and the ensuing discussion centered on ordering the books and the date of the next meeting.

Evangeline stood to write the name of the book and date on the large calendar she had hanging in the back room. As she finished scribbling it in, she heard a knock at the door leading to the hallway.

When she opened it, Denny stood in the hallway, one hand resting on the door frame, the other in the pockets of his worn blue jeans. His T-shirt strained across his chest and shoulders, and behind her she heard a faint sigh and a whispered, "Oh, yeah."

"Is everything okay?" she asked, trying not let Mia's reaction get to her.

Denny straightened as he looked past her to the group in the room. "Sorry. I didn't know you were busy. I can come another time."

"It's okay," she said, folding her arms over her chest. "We're just finishing up."

"I just…I just needed to borrow a couple of garbage bags." He gave her a crooked smile. "I forgot to pick 'em up when we were at the grocery store."

"I've got some here in the bookstore," she said,

e closed and locked the door of the bookstore, hurrying around the room, tidying and thumping pillows in a bid to channel her frustration with her father.

Why had Andy felt the need to go through Denny? Wh~~~~~ ~~~~talk to her himself?
~~~~~~~~~~~~~~~~~~~~~~~~~ ~~to~~ *face*

taking a quick step back, his smile creating an unwelcome reaction.

As she turned to get the bags, people were getting to their feet. Evangeline didn't make eye contact with Mia but could easily see her speculative look in her peripheral vision. It took Evangeline a few moments to find the bags and when she returned many of the women were leaving, walking past Denny, who stood aside, nodding and smiling at them.

Mia, the last one in the room, was hooking her purse over her shoulder. As she walked past Denny she gave him a quick smile. "Nice meeting you," she said, looking back at Evangeline again, giving her a discreet thumbs-up.

Ignoring her friend, Evangeline handed Denny the bags and he took them with a murmured thanks. But he didn't leave.

When Mia had disappeared down the end of the hallway, Denny turned back to Evangeline and smiled. "I thought I should tell you, I got another message from your dad. He asked me to let you know that he got a line on a new project. He said he'd be tied up for a couple of weeks for sure."

Evangeline felt her heart grow heavy, like a rock in her chest, as she just stared at Denny.

"He couldn't tell me himself?" she said, unable to keep the chill out of her voice.

Denny shrugged, his smile fading away. "He said he tried to call you—"

"He didn't try at all," she snapped. She was about to say more, but stopped, aware of Denny's puzzled look.

"I'm sorry," he said. "I just thought I would let you know."

Evangeline lifted her hand to stop his apology. "It's not your fault."

"Maybe not, but I am sorry," he said again, holding his hand out as if in a peace offering. "When I told him to call you himself, he said he tried, so I offered to tell you."

Evangeline heard the sympathetic note in his voice and, unable to stop herself, looked up at him.

In his dark eyes she caught a glimmer of sympathy.

He does have thick eyelashes, she thought. *And kind eyes.*

A small spark of longing was kindled in her and for a heartbeat she felt a connection to him.

Then she caught herself, brought reality into the situation and glanced away. Was she crazy?

Not hero material, she reminded herself. He was exactly like her father, which was the last thing she needed in her life right now.

Plus, he had a baby he had to take care of.

"Thanks for telling me," she said quietly, look-

ing away. Stepping back. "I'll try when I have the time."

"Another thing. I was wondering if you give me the name of a good babysitter. I n someone to watch Ella while I'm working. I can get ahold of either of m stuck."

Evangeline frowned. "I can't think of anyone off the top of my head, but I can ask Mia. She might have some ideas."

"That would be great," he said, blowing out his breath on a sigh. "I just...I don't know what to do. I've helped take care of my sisters, but not when they were babies."

Once again Evangeline felt sorry for him and his situation.

"Is Ella sleeping okay?" she asked.

Denny ran his hand over his head, messing his already tousled hair. "Yeah, and I just checked on her. Out like a light. Poor kid had a crazy day."

As did you, Evangeline thought, glancing up at him. She was disconcerted to find him looking at her. Once again their eyes locked and this time it wasn't sympathy she saw in them.

Then he pushed himself away from the door and shoved his hands into the back pockets of his worn blue jeans. "I better go."

She gave him a tight smile and waited until he closed the door across the hall behind him. Then

Because he's scared. He doesn't want to [see?]
you after disappointing you yet again.

Coward.

Evangeline quickly finished up then headed out of the room and up the stairs to her apartment above the store.

After her aunt had moved out, Evangeline had cleaned it out and put her own stuff in it. Now a pair of overstuffed white love seats sat across from each other, a mahogany coffee table between them. A grouping of narrow glass vases holding white-and-red gerbera daisies decorated the middle. A pink-and-white-striped easy chair was tucked into one corner beside the old fireplace, a lamp with a stained glass shade in shades of cream, gold and pink overlooking it. Beside the chair sat another low table holding a variety of books held up by gold bookends. The mantel of the fireplace held a couple of pictures. One of Evangeline and her mother. The other of her and her father. She didn't have one of the three of them.

Beyond the living room was the dining room

with its antique sideboard Eva ished in a distressed sage-gree the table and chairs.

had fin- atched

An old crocheted doily Evangeli at the thrift store covered the table, cased another collection of vas candles in varying shades of g

ound

spa

He'

A girlie place.

Her place.

Evangeline eased a kink out of her neck as she walked to her easy chair, ready to rid herself of the tension of the day. Then the phone sent out its harsh demand from the kitchen.

Evangeline sighed and glanced at the clock, wondering who would be calling this late.

"Hello? Evangeline speaking," she said, tucking the phone under her chin as she leaned her elbows on the counter.

"Hey, poppet, it's Dad."

In spite of her frustration with him, she couldn't help the skip of her heart or the lift of anticipation his voice gave her. "Hey, Dad," she said, trying to stifle her faint breathlessness.

"Sorry we didn't connect. I did try to call your cell but you weren't picking up."

"That's funny, I had my phone on me all day and I caught my other calls," she said, injecting a note of innocent surprise into her voice, unable to simply let his fib go unchallenged.

wrong number."

"Maybe I... a moment, then decided to let
She held... he said would cause her father
it go. ...ny of half-truths and evasive com-
to c... uld only make her angrier.
...th...
...d your messages from Denny, though,"

...s a great guy, isn't he?" her father said,
his hearty obtuseness making Evangeline shake
her head.

She didn't want to talk about Denny. He had
burst into her life and was already taking up too
much real estate in her thoughts.

"So what are you up to?" she asked.

_Besides not being here to do what you prom-
ised me you would years ago?_

She let the thought go unvoiced.

"On the road right now," he replied. "Busier
than a long-tailed cat in a room full of rocking
chairs. Just got a new contract. It will make all
the difference."

A too familiar refrain, she thought.

"I thought you said you were slowing down?"

Just six months ago another truck had side-
swiped him on an interstate and he had spun out
of control. The tractor had come away from the
trailer and rolled twice before coming to land
on the side of an embankment, mere feet from
where it plunged into a rocky gorge. The close

call started him talking about finishing the deal he'd promised her for years.

"I will. Once this job is done."

Evangeline pressed her lips together and glanced out the window beside her.

From this vantage point she could look over Main Street Hartley Creek with its brick buildings and wrought-iron lampposts, now decorated with hanging flowerpots. Beyond the town loomed the mountains cradling the valley.

She had seen this view for most of her life through the varying seasons yet she never grew tired of it. This store was her anchor; the only stability in her life. The past few years she had poured so much of her energy into it, clinging to her father's promise to sign it over to her. "And when this job is done should I rebook that lawyer's appointment?" she asked. There was a sharp edge to her voice.

The silence that followed her comment held a heaviness that carried over the phone line. Her father released a slow sigh and for a moment Evangeline thought she had pushed him too far.

"It's still my store, Evangeline," he said with quiet force.

She wanted to remind him that though it was his store now, it had once been his wife's store. And her mother had always promised that someday this store would be hers. Her father was only keeping her promise.

But she kept those comments tucked safely away. She heard testiness in his voice that only came out when he was stressed and she didn't want to push him when he was like that.

"I said I would sign the store over to you and I will," he continued. "I'm a man of my word, Evangeline. It will happen."

Trouble was, her father was a man of many words and she never knew which ones to believe and which ones to discard.

"Of course, Dad." She turned to lean back against the counter, looking over the apartment she had considered hers since she was nineteen.

"How is Denny making out? You show him the ranch like I asked?"

"Yeah. I did."

"Good. Good. He seems like a hard worker. I think he'll do well there between his trucking and ranching."

"I suppose."

"You heard anything from that Tyler guy? He see the light and decide to come back to you?"

Evangeline stifled a sigh. "Even if he did, I doubt I would take him back."

"He was good for you."

And how would you know? she wanted to ask.

"What did you think of Denny?" her father asked. "How are you getting on with him?"

"He just had a daughter from his dead ex-wife dropped onto his doorstep," Evangeline replied.

"Yeah. He told me he never knew about the baby."

Evangeline wasn't sure she believed Denny's protestations of ignorance. How could someone not know they have a child and why would his wife have kept that a secret?

"Where are you right now?" she asked, shifting to a safer topic.

"Great Falls heading over to Bonner's Ferry. That's where I met Denny. At a diner in Bonner's Ferry."

"Mmm-hmm," Evangeline said, keeping her responses noncommittal.

"We clicked right away. Got a lot in common. He reminds me of myself when I was younger."

And that was part of the problem.

"I see. Well, Dad, while I appreciate the call, it's late."

"Sounds like you're trying to get rid of your old man. You aren't going to tell me about the store?"

"It's been a long day." An interesting and challenging day, she wanted to add. "And I've an early start tomorrow." And no, she didn't want to tell him about the store in spite of his asking.

"You make sure to stay in touch. And be nice to Denny. He's one of a kind."

No, he's not, she wanted to say. *He's just like you.*

Which made him someone she didn't want to spend much time with. At all.

Chapter Five

Denny slowly pulled open the cupboard door, his heart skipping a beat as the hinges screeched. He waited a moment, holding his breath, his hands gripping the handle as his ears strained to hear something from Ella's room. He waited a full ten seconds.

Nothing.

He exhaled slowly, then gently set the glass in the cupboard. With one quick motion he shut the door, the hinges letting out another brief squawk.

He waited again. Again, nothing.

He glanced around the kitchen with bleary eyes. The dishes were finally done and the groceries he and Evangeline bought yesterday had been put away.

He had a few of his own boxes left to unpack and they stood by his bedroom door, mocking him. Ordinarily it would have taken him maybe another fifteen minutes to finish the job.

But ordinarily, he didn't have a toddler waking up every half hour, screaming, then taking another half an hour to settle down only to start the cycle again. Denny figured he had snatched a maximum of two hours' sleep the entire night.

The first few times he'd felt bad for the little munchkin. He'd walked and rocked and paced the floor for probably ten miles, trying to get her to sleep.

The whole while he did this he'd wondered if Ella had been the same way for Deb. For Lila. He struggled with his anger toward Deb for not letting him know. Toward Lila's parents for not contacting him.

He had snatched a few moments last night to text his sister Olivia, asking her to come and help him, but so far no answer.

He yawned as he stumbled over to the couch and fell onto it, fatigue dropping on him like a heavy blanket. But no sooner did his eyes close than a memory of Lila slipped into his mind. He shook his head and sent up a prayer for her soul. Lila hadn't gone with him to church when Denny had started going back. But she would listen to him when he read the Bible at dinnertime, the few times she was actually around. And she would bow her head when they prayed.

He eased out a sigh, his feelings a confusion of sorrow. Once again he felt a slow thrum of anger with Deb and her parents. Why hadn't they told him?

But in spite of his anger blended with his sorrow, exhaustion overtook him; his thoughts became jumbled and he fell into a troubled sleep.

Then a squawk resounded from the room beside him. Denny shot up, his heart thudding. The squawk soon became a whimper, which became a wail, which became a howl he was growing too acquainted with.

He glanced at the clock. Seven. He'd managed to grab a mere twenty more minutes of precious sleep.

Morning has broken, he thought.

He scrubbed at his face with his hands, his whiskers rasping on his calluses.

Do what comes next.

Yeah. Great. But what is next?

That question was answered for him when he stepped into the darkened room and bent over the crib to pick up a screaming, squirming baby. She was soaking wet from her knees to her chest. She flailed in his arms, tears slipping out from between scrunched-up eyes as her ever-increasing wails pierced his sleep-deprived ears.

"Easy, girl," he mumbled as, one-handed, he

rummaged through the bag of clothes Deb had given him.

But holding Ella was like trying to hold on to a baby calf. She squirmed and screamed and pushed at him with her hands.

Finally he managed to find a dry sleeper. He tossed it over his shoulder and tugged a diaper free from the bag he and Evangeline had bought yesterday.

He rushed back to the living room, her shrill cries creating an urgency to fix the problem, his shirt growing increasingly damp where she was pressing against him.

He laid her on the couch and tugged the zipper of her sleeper down. She squirmed, hit at him and turned over, sobbing all the while.

He tried to move her onto her back but she was amazingly strong for such a little thing. And she had a powerful and untiring set of lungs.

Above all this noise, he heard a knock at the door.

"Come in," he called, jumping up to open it and then stopping as he saw Ella twist around on the couch. He caught her just before she fell, hooked her over his arm and rushed to the door.

Evangeline stood in the doorway, a half smile curving her lips, her hair falling like a shining wave over the shoulders of a gauzy pink shirt.

"Everything okay?" she asked, her eyes holding his for a heart-stopping moment that maybe went on too long.

"Yeah. Well, no." He shifted Ella, turning so she was pressed against him again, making his shirt even damper. "I'm trying to change her."

"Sounds like you've been having some trouble. Do you want some help?"

His usual independence came to the fore and he wanted to say no. He didn't want Evangeline entering the mess his life had become, but practicality trumped pride.

"If you're not busy?" he asked, raising his voice above Ella's cries.

She shook her head. "Store doesn't open until ten. I've got some time."

He felt as if a rock had been lifted off his back. "Thanks. Thanks so much."

Evangeline took the crying baby out of his arms, walked over to the couch and laid her gently on the blanket. With quick and efficient movements she stripped the sleeper and diaper off, attached a clean diaper and threaded Ella's chubby and flailing hands and feet into the clean sleeper.

"Could you get some milk in a sippy cup for her?" Evangeline said above Ella's continuing cries.

Thankful to have some direction, Denny hurried to the kitchen and quickly got the cup ready.

He drummed his fingers on the counter as the microwave hummed. Before it was finished beeping he had the cup out and rushed back to the couch, handing the cup to Evangeline.

Ella reached out for the cup with her chubby hands, her cries immediately ceasing as she shoved the cup into her mouth. She tipped it back, her eyes closing, tears still glimmering on her thick eyelashes.

"She was thirsty," Evangeline murmured in the blissful quiet that followed.

"She had about two cups of milk during the night," Denny said, sinking into the chair across from Evangeline.

"Was she up a lot?"

"Most of the night." Denny suppressed a yawn, but another one followed, almost cracking his jaw.

Evangeline gave him a sympathetic smile, which made her even more lovely. Sitting on the couch, her arms curved around Ella, her long, wavy hair slipping across her cheek, she exuded beauty and grace.

Denny shook off his reaction. He and Evangeline were on completely different planes. He had a five-year plan and even if he didn't have his plan, he now had Ella to deal with. He had no room for anyone else.

Ella finished drinking the cup of milk, but her

once-greedy gulps slowed with each suck until her eyes shut and the cup slowly slipped out of her grasp.

"I think she's falling asleep," Evangeline whispered, catching the cup and setting it aside.

"Awesome." Denny released another yawn, then lifted a hand in apology. "Sorry. Didn't get much sleep last night." And though he hadn't planned to drive today, he still had a bunch of work to get done.

Obviously that wasn't happening.

Evangeline leaned back into the couch, her arms curled around Ella's slack body, her chin resting on Ella's blond curls.

She's a natural, Denny thought. *A beautiful, natural mother.* He blinked the romantic notion away then shook his head to settle his thoughts. He sucked in a slow breath, focusing on what he had to do next.

"Hey, you look done in," Evangeline said quietly, pulling his attention back to her. "Why don't you lie down? Grab some sleep."

Sleep. The word tantalized, but he couldn't expect Evangeline to take care of his little girl while he dozed off.

"No. I have too much to do."

"Look," she reasoned, "I know you've got stuff to do but you won't be able to if you are exhausted. Just grab an hour, maybe two. I don't mind helping you out right now."

He stared at her, reason fighting with the weariness that made his thoughts fuzzy and incoherent.

"I insist," she continued. "I don't want you operating on minimal sleep while driving a gravel truck around the county. I'm just thinking of my community here."

He didn't have to drive today, but she seemed determined to help. And she was right. He was no good if he didn't grab some sleep.

"Okay. Just for a few minutes." He dropped back into the chair, put his stockinged feet up on the coffee table and laid his head back.

He closed his eyes and as he did he hoped his socks didn't have any holes in them, and then sleep tugged him down into darkness.

Evangeline pursed her lips, looking over at Denny, his head off to one side, his features relaxed as he slept.

This was not how she thought this would turn out. Denny was supposed to have gone to his bedroom and lain on his bed, not dropped into a chair right across from her, looking all vulnerable, tousled and charming.

She looked down at Ella, who also lay sleeping in her arms, her mouth open ever so slightly, showing tiny, pearly white teeth.

Like father, like daughter, she thought, shifting her own weight to try to get up. She would lay the baby in her crib and make her exit.

But as soon as she moved, Ella's eyes flew open. Evangeline sank back into the soft couch, cradling the baby close, praying she would fall asleep again.

Not that she felt she had the right to ask God for anything.

Since her father had told her he would sign the store over to her, she had started making plans for the things she wanted to change. A corner for young mothers to sit and read to their kids. An expanded section for kids with educational and fun toys. The plans had kept her busy, and in the past year, Sundays had been taken up with meeting potential suppliers and attending various conventions showcasing the products she wanted to carry.

Church and her faith had become less of a priority.

Maybe her father's reneging on his deal was a punishment for neglecting her faith.

She shook that thought off. She knew God didn't work that way, but she couldn't stifle the guilt that always accompanied gentle reprimands from Mia, Renee or Emma when they asked her why she wasn't in church.

She stole another glance at Denny, who did go to church. In that way, he was unlike her father.

He had moved his head, his chin now resting on one shoulder. He looked vulnerable with his stubble-shaded jaw, his disheveled hair and his sleep-slackened features. His eyelashes lay like a dark fringe, making him look even more appealing.

She thought of the moment when he'd opened the door and their eyes had met. How her heart had done that stupid little hop.

She glanced down at his daughter in her arms; a visual reminder of the tangled relationships Denny dragged behind him. A child he knew nothing about from a divorced wife.

Denny was handsome, all right, but oh, so wrong for her.

Evangeline had already made too many wrong choices. She wasn't letting herself fall into that trap again.

Remember Tyler. Remember your father.

And with that litany running through her head, Evangeline focused her attention on the helpless, abandoned baby in her arms.

Half an hour later Denny still slept and Evangeline dared to slowly get to her feet. She tiptoed past Denny, then into Ella's room. Carefully, slowly, she laid the little girl in her crib, waited with bated breath while Ella shifted, sighed and then drifted back off to sleep.

A few minutes later Evangeline was back in the cramped room she called her office, catching up on neglected bookwork.

She turned on her computer, smiling as she always did at the picture that greeted her. Each day a different cover from a different historical romance showed up on her desktop as her wallpaper.

Today an elegant duke stared back at her, his one hand clutching the front of his waistcoat, the other resting on a walking stick. His dark hair, á la Mr. Darcy, was fashionably rumpled and his eyes held a glint of humor. He was the hero of the book she had just finished when Denny strode into her store.

He even looked like Denny, come to think of it.

She shook the silly notion off. Denny was no hero. Not in her life.

Half an hour later the bills were paid and she had reconciled her checking account, pleased to see the final amount. Business was good and with the expansion—

She cut that thought off with a pang of sorrow blended with anger. The expansion wasn't happening as long as her father still held ownership of the store.

She pushed herself away from her computer desk and a book fell with a thump onto the floor behind the desk. As she bent to retrieve the book she felt a sliver of guilt.

Her Bible.

Her poor, neglected Bible.

She picked it up and sat back in her chair looking down at it. How long since she had read it?

Why not now?

She had to open the store in a few minutes, she told herself. She was supposed to return a call to one of her suppliers and unpack that new shipment of books that had arrived yesterday. She didn't have the time.

But even as she formulated that thought a nagging guilt followed it. And a memory.

Her mother would read a Children's Bible to her every night before she went to bed. In fact the Bible Evangeline now held on her lap had belonged to her mother. Her mother had always told her that God loved her like a father loved his own child.

Evangeline closed her eyes, frustration mingled with a wave of sorrow coursed through her. Maybe not the best example.

She ignored the guilt and set the Bible aside. *Maybe another time,* she thought. She got up, walked to the door and unlocked it.

Then she went to the storeroom and pulled out

her latest shipment. A faint sense of anticipation sang through her at the thought of the brand-new books waiting to be inventoried and shelved.

An hour and five customers later, she was partially through the box when she heard the door of the back room open and a voice calling her name.

Her heart lifted and she caught herself smoothing her hair.

Denny stepped cautiously into the store, looking around.

"Over here," Evangeline said, getting to her feet.

His hair, tamed and brushed, still glistened from his shower and his strong jaw shone from his shave. He wore a plain brown shirt tucked into new blue jeans.

"Hey. Thanks so much for putting Ella to sleep," he said, his slow-release smile making her heart quiver in spite of her resolve.

"Yeah. No problem." Evangeline ran her hands down her thighs, nodding. "Is she still sleeping?"

"Out like a light. I was wondering what I should give her when she wakes up again. She hasn't had anything but that cup of milk."

"Probably some warm cereal. Just follow the instructions. Maybe blueberries, as well?" Evangeline wasn't sure, either, but threw the suggestions out anyway.

"That sounds good." He shifted his weight as

he slipped his hands into the front pockets of his jeans. "I better let you get back to work," he said, taking a step back and giving her an apologetic smile. "I shouldn't leave Ella alone too long. And about that babysitter...I'm thinking I would prefer if they could come to the apartment to take care of her, but I'd be willing to take her somewhere, too. Whatever works."

Evangeline nodded and, as Denny left, sorrow stirred in her soul. Poor Ella. Only here a day and she was already getting shuffled around. Too familiar.

Half an hour later the first box of books was inventoried and the store was still quiet, so Evangeline started making a list of prospective babysitters.

Then, whenever she had a spare moment, she phoned someone on the list.

By the time she was ready to close the store that evening, between dealing with customers and finishing unpacking the books, Evangeline figured she must have made about twenty-seven calls. She had started with her friends, then the book club, then customers. She'd even swallowed her guilt and called people from church that she hadn't seen in ages.

Trouble was, there was no one available to work all day and, potentially, into the evening if Denny was late. Evangeline knew how trucking worked. Breakdowns and delays meant Denny could show up anywhere from five-thirty to nine at night.

She could have created a hodgepodge schedule of babysitters but Evangeline knew that she would be in charge of following through if one couldn't make it.

Why don't you do it?

Evangeline dismissed the question as soon as it formulated in her mind. There was no way she could take care of a baby. She had a business to run.

You could have her here in the store. Just like your aunt did when school was out.

But she had been a child of eight. And she had kept herself entertained as her aunt ran the store.

However, the pernicious suggestion wouldn't leave her alone. She pressed her fingers to her temples as sympathy for Ella battled with practicality. She easily remembered that perfect moment this morning in Denny's apartment, the little girl cuddled up against her; a soft, sweet weight.

And Denny sleeping across from her—

She gave her head a shake and focused her thoughts on Ella. That precious little girl didn't have anyone going to bat for her right now. Her mother was dead and her father, Denny, had his business to take care of.

Ella's plight reminded Evangeline of her own youth. A busy father, no mother and the only person to take care of her was a well-meaning but somewhat aggrieved aunt.

But did she want to entangle herself so quickly and deeply in Denny's life?

It's for Ella, she reminded herself.

She walked to the door of the store, locked it up and flipped the Open sign to Closed. Then she walked through the back, across the hall and knocked on Denny's door.

She wasn't sure if he was home. She thought she had heard him leave a while back, but only seconds after she knocked, the door opened and Denny stood there looking rough and ragged. He must have had a busy day.

But in spite of that, he still exuded an appeal she had a hard time ignoring.

"Hey, there," he said with a welcoming smile that niggled at her equilibrium. "Come on in."

"Is Ella up?"

He shook his head. "I took her out with me this afternoon. Had to meet my one driver. She fussed the whole time, so thank goodness she's asleep now."

Evangeline only nodded.

"So did you come to tell me you found a babysitter?" The hopeful note in his voice accompanied by an expectant look increased her burden.

She hesitated. She could still back out, she thought, her mind ticking over the possible scenarios for Ella and Denny. But there was only one she could follow through on.

"I decided I would take care of her. I'm right here and if you're late, I can bring her to your apartment. All her stuff is here…her food and clothes. I figured it was the easiest solution."

She stopped the flow of words spilling out of her mouth. It was as if she was trying to convince herself as much as him.

"You couldn't find anyone else?"

"You don't think I can do it?" A faintly defensive note entered Evangeline's voice.

Denny held his hands up. "I didn't mean that the way it sounded. You're busy with your store and I don't want to impose. I thought you could've found somebody—"

"The store is not complicated work. And I think most of the customers will understand the situation." Hopefully. So much depended on how Ella behaved.

Denny scratched his head with a forefinger. "Are you sure?"

No, she wasn't sure, but until she found someone who was able and willing to make the time commitment, she couldn't see any way around it.

"I am. I did find a young girl who would be able to either watch Ella for a couple of hours in the afternoon or help me in the store, which would give me a break and allow her to have a quiet nap here in the apartment."

Denny still didn't seem convinced.

"Look, I don't mind doing it," Evangeline continued. "I wouldn't offer if I did. Besides, it's temporary. You did say your sister was coming."

Denny's sigh was one of reluctant resignation but Evangeline knew better than he did that there were no other options. "That's right, but the minute it's too much—"

"I'll let you know," she assured him.

He nodded, sighing again. He looked exhausted. For a moment she wanted to offer him and Ella supper, but that was blurring boundaries she needed to keep in place.

"So I thought I would let you know what was up," Evangeline continued, "and find out what time you will be leaving in the morning."

"I can take care of her tomorrow. I just have to get my contracts in order and make sure my trucks are moved. But I do have to head out Friday at about eight."

She was surprised. Her father always started much earlier. "That would work well. I'll stop by to pick her up then."

Denny massaged his neck. "You've taken a huge load off my shoulders," he said. "But I'm still not comfortable with this."

Neither was she. "It's just for now," she replied. "I'll keep looking."

A cry from the bedroom made him spin around, his thankful smile dropping away. "Sounds like Ella is awake. I gotta go."

Evangeline took an unconscious step toward the door as Denny strode toward the bedroom, then stopped herself. Denny had this.

She was entangled enough in their story.

Chapter Six

Denny shot a quick glance at the clock on his truck's dash as he pulled into the parking spot behind his apartment. Six-thirty. An hour later than he'd told Evangeline in his text message he would arrive.

Guilt and frustration wove themselves tightly around his stomach. While taking care of Ella yesterday, he'd managed to arrange the move of his trucks. Today he'd started hauling again. Two hours later than he'd wanted to, but he couldn't expect Evangeline to take care of Ella from his usual six in the morning to the end of the day.

His other trucks were still hauling but he'd cut himself short by one run. The job was farther away from Hartley Creek than he'd thought and the run was longer than he had been told. He was assured that an adjustment would be made in the contract, but it still meant he wasn't back when he had told Evangeline he would be.

He rotated his neck, trying to ease the tension gripping it ever since Ella had been dropped on his doorstep.

A kid. He had a kid.

And a woman he barely knew was taking care of her.

He stared blankly at the brick wall in front of him, trying to still the faint panic that crept up every time he thought of Ella.

How was he supposed to work that little girl into his crazy, busy life? He had always wanted children someday, but within the bounds of a stable marriage. That Lila couldn't get pregnant had been difficult at first but as the marriage fell apart, he'd seen it as a mixed blessing.

Now he had a child, but no wife. And no stability in his life, either.

His phone chimed and he glanced down to see who was texting. Olivia. Finally. He swiped his thumb across the screen and a text message popped up.

Got your text, the note on the screen read. Sorry. Can't come for a week or so. But need a few $$s.

He felt a niggle of resentment. Olivia seemed to contact him only when she needed something. Usually money.

Will send it if you come to Hartley Creek. I need your help, he texted back. There. See what she does with that.

What help? I'm working.

He shook his head, then texted, Just come to Hartley Creek and I'll tell you. Olivia wasn't making a lot of money tree planting if she needed money from him. She could quit her job and help him out.

He waited to see what she would say to that, but no reply was zinging back to him.

Wasn't that typical? If his sisters needed his help they were quick enough to come to him, but if he needed something they usually had some excuse.

He laid his head back against the seat of his truck and closed his eyes.

"Dear Lord," he prayed, "help me to get through this. I'm completely at a loss here. I need Your help. I don't know how to take care of a little girl and I've got a hundred things to do. I can't count on Evangeline to take over. Please help me let go of my worries and trust in You. Please bring peace into my life."

He waited a moment, then slowly got out of the truck. Too many times he had prayed that same prayer for peace in his life. Maybe someday it would be answered.

He opened the back door of the apartment,

stepped inside and did a double take. Trying to get Ella fed this morning and ready to take to Evangeline had been a whirlwind of activity. He had left the place looking as though a tornado had spun through it.

But everything was neatly in place. No trace of tossed clothes and dirty breakfast dishes.

Had Evangeline done all this, too?

He felt a mixture of thankfulness and extra obligation and he wasn't sure what to do with his emotions. He wasn't comfortable having someone help him.

He pulled his boots off and set them aside in the back entrance then hurried through the apartment to the hallway and knocked on the back door of the store.

He waited a moment, then he heard footsteps, the sound of giggling, and the door opened.

Evangeline stood, holding Ella on one hip, her hair swept to one side. She was grinning and Ella, solemn little Ella, was laughing, batting at a little stuffed teddy bear Evangeline was holding in her other hand.

"Hey, there," he said, grinning at the sight of Ella laughing and the sight of Evangeline's smile. "I'm sorry I'm late."

She shrugged, her eyes flicking from him to Ella, touching the tip of her nose with the face of the bear. "That's the life of truckers" was her enigmatic reply.

"So, how did it go?" He looked past her to the room where Evangeline and her friends had gathered that one night. Comfy chairs circled the edges of the room, but some had been pushed aside to make room for a portable crib. "I see you took the crib from the apartment."

"I did. Sorry. Ella was tired this morning so I got the crib and laid her down back here." Evangeline shot him another quick glance. "I had to go into the apartment. I, uh, also took the liberty of cleaning up. I had to get Ella lunch and...well—"

He held his hand up to stop her midapology. "You're the landlord and I appreciate you cleaning up. You didn't have to do that."

Ella giggled again, then looked over at him. As soon as she saw he was looking at her, she buried her head against Evangeline's shoulder, her chubby arms snaking around her neck.

He couldn't blame her. He probably looked rough. The gravel pit was dusty and dirty and he hadn't stopped to clean up.

"Hey, girl," he said, reaching for Ella. "We need to go."

But Ella didn't lift her head and started to whimper.

Looked like it would be another long night, he thought with a stab of dismay.

"Why don't you bring her crib back to your apartment and I'll take her across," Evangeline offered, shifting her weight as Ella still clung to her.

Denny felt as if he should protest, but it didn't look as though Ella was going to him right away so he collapsed the portable crib and brought it back to Ella's room and set it up again.

Evangeline was shushing Ella, who'd begun to whimper again as soon as she'd entered the apartment.

"Not such good memories for her here," Denny said, coming out of her bedroom.

He held his hands out to take Ella from Evangeline again. Evangeline glanced from Ella to him and then with a melancholy smile eased her over to Denny.

But Ella leaned away from him toward Evangeline, throwing him off balance, her whimpers turning to cries of anguish.

"Hey, baby," Denny said, turning away from Evangeline, patting her back as he struggled to settle her, wondering why she was so upset as soon as he held her.

Maybe the little girl had sensed he hadn't wanted her when Deb dropped her off.

While her cries filled the apartment he rocked her back and forth, drawing on his limited experience with his younger sisters, who had all been older than Ella when he'd taken care of them. But he didn't think Ella would appreciate being tossed in the air or being pushed around on the floor while he growled like a wolf the way he had for his sisters.

Ella kept twisting in his arms, looking past him toward Evangeline, tears streaming down her cheeks, sobs shaking her body.

"Here. I'll take her," Evangeline said. "She's probably hungry. She hasn't had her supper yet."

"Right. Of course." Denny released his red-faced and upset daughter with a sense of guilty relief.

He ran his hands through his dusty hair then hurried over to the kitchen, yanking open the cupboard. "So, the turkey and sweet potato?" he asked, pulling out a jar for Evangeline's approval as Ella's cries subsided.

"That sounds good. Maybe some fruit with that?"

He grabbed a jar with a picture of blueberries on it and a smiling baby who seemed to mock him. Ella had settled down, but she was still sniffling.

"Her bowl is in the dishwasher," Evangeline said.

"Right." Denny washed his hands, found the bowl and set it on the counter. He hurriedly scooped the food into the various partitions then shoved it in the microwave, remembering from last night not to make it too hot. He pushed the right buttons, then turned to see what Ella was doing.

Evangeline was on the couch, Ella parked on her lap while she chewed on the teddy bear.

"So. How was she today?" he asked as the microwave hummed behind him.

"Really good. I brought her here for lunch and she ate well. She had a good nap this afternoon."

Denny nodded as he watched Evangeline playing with Ella, feeling very challenged and, if he was truly honest with himself, very confused. On the one hand he felt guilty that Evangeline was taking care of his daughter and on the other he wasn't even sure how he felt about Ella. Shouldn't a father have an immediate connection to his own flesh and blood?

And what if she wasn't?

Your name is on the birth certificate.

And her age lined up with those few weeks when Denny thought he and Lila would try to make their marriage work.

He had to accept that she was his daughter. And the sooner he did, the sooner he could figure out where his life was going next.

"How was your first day on the job?" Evangeline asked, tossing her hair to one side to look up at him, her easy smile creating a sense of anticipation.

He couldn't help a crooked grin. "Good. Busy. Sorry again about being late."

"Hey. I'm the daughter of a trucker. I know all about late nights and missed appointments."

Her voice held the tiniest edge, which made him wonder, again, about her relationship with Andy.

The microwave beeped and Evangeline got up to put Ella in her high chair. Denny pulled the food out and then dragged a kitchen chair toward the high chair, sat and set Ella's food on the tray.

"Hey, little girl, time for supper," he said.

Her lower lip quivered as he scooped up some food on a spoon and got it in her mouth. Then Ella spit, spraying the turkey and sweet potato over the front of Denny's shirt.

"Okay, let's try that again," Denny said with a forced smile, scooping up another spoonful.

This time he managed to snatch the spoon back before she spit again. Ella reached her arms up, looking past Denny to where Evangeline stood behind them.

"I don't think she likes me," Denny said.

"It might help if you talk to her," Evangeline suggested, coming to stand beside them.

Denny knew he had to keep his focus on Ella, but he was distracted by the lingering scent of Evangeline's perfume. It smelled like fresh air and open meadows. She was wearing a draped sweater and a swirly kind of skirt that flowed when she walked.

A princess, just as Andy had said.

He swallowed, blaming his wandering attention on the loneliness that caught at him from time to time. Though he yearned to be on his own, and yearned for the peace that might bring him, there were times where he also yearned for companionship. A woman to share his life in every sense of the word.

He caught himself short, forced himself to stop his thoughts right there. He didn't have any space in his life for a woman.

"So what do I talk to her about?" he asked as he gave Ella another spoonful of food. Thankfully this time she took it. "I doubt she follows sports or where the Dow Jones is."

Evangeline's throaty laugh threatened his previous resolve. "Doesn't matter what you talk about. The sound of your voice is enough to connect with her."

He nodded while managing to get another spoonful of food past Ella's lips. However, he wasn't about to engage in conversation with a toddler in front of Evangeline.

"Looks like you've got things under control," Evangeline said. "If you don't need me anymore, then I'll leave you two."

Denny turned to give her a grateful smile. "I can't tell you how much I appreciate your help. Make sure you keep track of your hours."

Evangeline waved her hand at him in a gesture of dismissal. "Don't worry about that. Did you hear from your sister?"

Guilt and anger stabbed at him. "Yeah. She can't come yet." Just then his cell phone went off.

He yanked it directly out of his pocket. Maybe it was Olivia. Maybe she had changed her mind. He glanced at the phone, curious. Not Olivia but Martha, the wife of the man who was holding his yearlings for him.

He was about to answer when his phone buzzed again with a text message. Again, not Olivia but one of his truck drivers.

"You're busy, let me feed her." Evangeline took the spoon from his hand and shooed him out of his chair. Reluctantly he got up and let her take over as he answered his phone. The text he would deal with later.

"Hello, Martha. How are you?" he said as he walked away from Ella and Evangeline.

"I'm okay but I have bad news." Her deep sigh coupled with her words created a clench of dread deep in his stomach. Of course. When, in the past few days, had he heard good news?

"What's up? The yearlings okay?" he asked, his hand tightening its grip on his cell phone.

"They're fine. But Bart isn't. He's had a heart attack and is in the hospital."

"Oh, no. I'm so sorry to hear that."

"It's been rough, but he's okay now. Trouble is, the doctor told him to slow down. And that means he can't take care of your yearlings anymore. They'll have to be moved right away."

Denny dropped his head back, staring unseeingly at the ceiling as if calling down divine intervention. He pulled in a long, slow breath, then another.

"I'm not ready for them yet," he said, stifling the rising sense of panic that seemed to be his constant companion since he'd come to Hartley Creek.

His supposed place of refuge and quiet.

"Well, I'm sorry, but Bart can't do the work anymore. Those yearlings have to be moved. In fact, I'll probably have to sell the cows, too."

Denny forced his spinning brain to slow down. *Think. Break it down.*

"Let me make a few calls and I'll get back to you. And say hi to Bart. Tell him to get better soon."

"I will, and again, I'm sorry, but you'll need to do this in the next two days."

"Of course. I'll see what I can do." Denny murmured another platitude and ended the call. He then checked his text message. It was Carlos telling him that he was taking care of oil changes on Denny's trucks.

"That didn't sound good," Evangeline said.

Denny turned to her, not sure he wanted to dump this on her. His life was a steady progression from bad to worse to disaster.

"So, sounds like you've got more work ahead of you," Evangeline said as she finished giving Ella her food.

Denny knew he couldn't keep it from her. "I've got to move my cows in the next two days."

"Will you be able to? I thought the fences on the ranch needed work," she said, taking a damp cloth and quickly wiping Ella's face.

"They do. I'll have to buy hay to feed them in the corrals until I get that done. And I don't know where I'm going to get the hay." And he had to run his gravel hauling business and try to keep Ella happy. He glanced over at his daughter, who was watching him again, her expression as solemn as a judge.

Fail on all counts, Denny thought, catching his lower lip between his teeth.

Break it down. Break it down. What's the next step?

"Shall I get Ella ready for bed?" Evangeline asked.

Denny was already so deeply indebted to her he could never pay her back. "No. She's my daughter. I'll take care of her."

Evangeline nodded as she tidied up the remainders of Ella's food. "Then I'll leave you alone."

"Thanks again," Denny said, giving her a weary smile. "I can't begin to let you know how much I appreciate your help."

"That's what neighbors do," she said with an airy wave of her hand. She patted Ella on the cheek then left.

As she closed the door an eerie quiet fell on the apartment.

He looked over at Ella, who was staring at him, her lower lip quivering.

Please, don't start crying.

Then he thought of what Evangeline had told him.

"So I'm supposed to talk to you," he said to Ella as he picked her up out of the high chair. "Though I kind of think it will be a one-sided conversation. Sort of like talking to Steve, my truck driver. He doesn't listen too well, but hey, he shows up and knows how to double clutch like who knows what."

Ella's lip stopped quivering and she blinked at him.

Guess Evangeline was right.

"You know, babe, it's just you and me," he continued. "I don't know why your mom or grandparents didn't tell me about you, but you're here now."

He carried her to the bedroom to get a clean sleeper. "So now I need to change you for the night and hopefully you'll go to bed and sleep like a trucker. Because sleeping like a baby isn't working too well for you." He was taken aback as he unbuttoned the little pink dress she wore. He didn't remember seeing it in the suitcase he had unpacked. "Did you have this when you came?" he asked Ella, who was chewing on her fist, her dark eyes latched on to his as if still trying to figure out who he was. "I don't recognize it. Looks brand-new."

He shrugged and set it aside. "Not that I have time to solve that mystery. I have to find a way to move my cows and run my trucks and take care of you. Though it seems that Auntie Evangeline is helpful there. Trouble is, we're both strangers to her. And I kind of think her first impression of me wasn't great, though she seems to have warmed up. A bit. Kind of like you." He grinned as Ella blew a spit bubble, holding her clasped hands in the air. "See, you just need to get to know me. Though my life is kind of like a truck without brakes on a runaway lane. Just going, going with no control." He sighed as he changed her diaper, thankful she was quiet. So he kept talking.

"All my life I've prayed that I would get married and have kids and live on a ranch. Trouble was, I kind of thought it would come as a package. Not piecemeal like this." He zipped up her sleeper then stood her up in front of him, her brown, heavily lashed eyes looking back at him with an expression that tugged at a memory.

Was he seeing things or did Ella resemble his sister Adrianna? He caught a glimpse of his sister in the dimple in Ella's cheek, the narrow bridge of her nose and the curl of her mouth.

"Hey, are you smiling at me?" He jiggled her and to his surprise, her mouth broke into a full-fledged smile. "You are smiling. You think I'm funny?"

He was rewarded with a burbling giggle that caused a peculiar curl in his stomach. He grinned back at her as she giggled again.

Then he took a chance and pulled her close. To his surprise and shock, she didn't resist. And then, after a moment, she laid her head against his shoulder. Her cheek was warm, soft and tender.

In that moment of connection, Denny felt his defenses melt like snow in the sunshine.

He patted her back, surprised at the affection coursing through him.

With a gentle laugh, he carefully got to his feet and walked to the kitchen. He poured milk into her cup with one hand and set it in the microwave. While it hummed, he pulled his head back to look at Ella, who still lay cuddled up against him. "So, babe, you got any ideas of what I should do with the gravel trucks? No? How about the cows?"

She turned her head at the sound of his voice and gave him another slow smile.

He laid his chin on her head and released a gentle sigh.

"If you come up with any ideas, let me know. I got a ton of phone calls to make to corral this new mess in my life. I had to hire a new trucker and get Carlos to manage the business. I won't make as much, but it will give me more time for you and the ranch," he said with a light sigh.

The microwave beeped and a few moments later he sat back on the couch, his feet up on the table, his arms curled around Ella's soft, cuddly warmth as she sucked back her milk. She stared up at him, smiled around the spout of the cup and then returned to her vigorous drinking.

He laughed as he gave her a quick hug, and for

the first time since he'd come to Hartley Creek, he felt a welcome peace steal over him.

Evangeline was right. Things would come together.

But even as thoughts of Evangeline and the faint attraction he felt for her slipped into his mind, he felt a hook in his heart. He had a little girl and a life that was a jumble of half-baked plans and work.

He had nothing to give a woman like her.

Don't even go there, he thought, looking at Ella. *She's not the woman for you and you're not the man for her.*

Not now, not ever.

Chapter Seven

"She is adorabubble." Renee Albertson curled her hands around her mug of coffee and gave Ella a quick smile.

Ella banged a wooden spoon on the table of her wooden high chair, netting her a few more grins from the other patrons of Mug Shots, a local coffee shop where Evangeline had agreed to meet her friend Renee to help plan her wedding.

It was Monday morning and the buzz of conversation ebbed and flowed around them as Evangeline sipped at her cup of herbal tea.

"How long do you think you can take care of her?" Renee asked, concern edging her voice.

Evangeline handed Ella another piece of blueberry scone, which she shoved into her mouth, crumbs flying.

"I don't know. I said I would help for now, because I can't find anyone willing or able to take care of her for the length of time Denny will be working."

"Poor kid," Renee said, cutting up one of her own grapes and setting it on Ella's tray. "What a business, getting dumped on a complete stranger. Good thing she's so young."

"Yeah, but she was plenty upset the first couple of days." Evangeline easily remembered Ella's heart-wrenching sobs when Denny's sister-in-law had dropped her off with Denny. "But she's getting better. Aren't you, my little muffin?" Evangeline said, giving Ella another smile and another piece of scone.

Renee sat back, a pensive look on her face as she twirled a lock of auburn hair around her finger. "You better be careful you don't burn out, my friend," she said with a somber tone. "You've got your plans for the store—"

"Plans I might have to shelve, since I doubt Andy is signing the store over to me anytime soon." She smiled to counteract the bitter note in her voice. "And how is your mother doing in that therapy program?" she asked, changing the subject. She didn't want to think about what she'd do if Andy never signed the store over to her. It was too scary to imagine that empty future. "Do they think her spinal injury will heal enough for her to walk again?"

Renee's smile lit up her face as she latched on

to Evangeline's change in topic. "She plans on walking down the aisle when she marries Zach's father. She was hinting at a double wedding with me and Zach, but I told her Zach and I didn't want to overshadow her special day."

"Two weddings are more exciting," Evangeline said, trying not to allow a hint of envy to creep into her voice. "So now that we decided on colors and a venue, when can you meet with Mia to talk about flowers?"

"Next week, and then I guess I'll have to contact Larissa about using the Morrisey Creek Inn." Renee gave Evangeline an enigmatic smile. "So, enough about the wedding. Why don't you tell me more about Ella's father? He seems like a nice guy."

Evangeline ignored her friend's comment and the underlying expectation in Renee's voice. She didn't want to talk about Denny. He was most definitely not the type of man she wanted to get involved with.

Then someone stopped at their table.

Evangeline looked up at Captain Jeff Deptuck, who stood beside the table, holding a take-out coffee cup. He wore his fireman's uniform—dark pants and shirt with the logo of the Hartley Creek Fire Department on his shoulder. Very official.

"So, Miss Evangeline, what have you been

keeping from your friends at book club?" he asked, pointing his coffee cup at Ella.

"She's Denny Norquest's little girl," Evangeline replied. "I'm taking care of her while he gets his gravel trucks ready."

"Is he the guy who showed up at the end of book club the other night?"

"Yes. He lives behind the store. In my father's old apartment."

Jeff gave her a sly wink. "Handy."

Evangeline ignored his insinuation. "Is there anything I can help you with?"

"Just wondering how I can get a copy of that book we're doing for book club. You don't have any at the store."

"The warehouse is still out of it," said Evangeline.

"I think Angie is finished hers," Renee broke in with a sly look.

Jeff nodded slowly, considering this piece of information, a slow grin spreading across his face. "I'll have to check that out." He saluted them with his coffee cup and left.

"A man with a mission," Renee said. She turned to Evangeline. "He's a great guy. A fireman. A hero."

"But he's got a thing for Angie," Evangeline said. "And I'm not interested. Still getting over Tyler."

"You were never into Tyler enough to have much to get over," Renee scolded. "It wasn't a matter of if you would break up, it was a matter of when. Besides, he was never the hero type."

"Heroes are few and far between," Evangeline agreed with a heavy sigh.

"And then there's Denny."

Evangeline shook her head so fast, her hair came loose from the clip that swept it to one side of her face. "He's definitely not hero material."

"I saw him in church yesterday."

And why had her friend made that particular conversational leap?

"And you weren't," Renee gently added.

Evangeline lifted her shoulder in a vague shrug as she realized where Renee was going. "I was catching up on bookkeeping and canceling some of the orders I made for my so-called expansion."

"Pastor Blacketer had a good sermon. You should have been there," Renee chided in a way that only a good friend could. "You attended church at one time. Before Tyler. Why don't you come again?"

"I've just been busy with my plans for the store. Conferences, phone calls." Her excuses sounded lame, even to her own ears. She knew there was an emptiness in her soul she'd been trying to fill by keeping busy with the store. But of late the void had grown larger. Deeper.

She knew it was a yearning for the God she'd once had a close relationship with.

"You could still come," Renee urged in her quiet, persistent way.

Before Evangeline could form another excuse, her phone buzzed. When she saw Denny's name on the call display, she felt an unwelcome flare of anticipation. She lowered her head as she answered the phone, hoping her hair would cover her reaction.

"Hello, what can I do for you?" she asked, keeping her tone formal.

"How's Ella behaving for you?"

His concern for his daughter was surprising and touching. "She's sitting here eating a blueberry scone. Renee is feeding her grapes."

"Sounds like you're giving her a well-balanced breakfast," Denny said, his teasing tone increasing the warmth in her cheeks.

"We try."

"I was wondering if you talked to the people staying in the house on the ranch," he continued.

Yesterday he had called her to ask about moving to the house earlier so he could be there when the cows arrived.

"I called them last night," she said, turning away from Renee, who seemed far too interested in her conversation. "I told them I would give them a month's free rent in the apartment if they vacated the house earlier, but they preferred a refund. They're dropping the keys off at the store this afternoon. When are the cows coming?"

"Tonight. I arranged for a truck to drop them off." Once again she heard a heaviness in his voice that made her feel sorry for him.

"But what are you going to feed them? You said you had to fix the fences before you could put them out into pasture."

"I'll have to take tomorrow off and hope the cows don't get out before that."

She was about to say something when she heard the squawk of his trucker's radio and the fuzzy sound of someone talking.

"Sounds like someone else needs to talk to you," she said. "I'll see you later."

As she ended the call, Evangeline dropped her phone into her purse and turned to see Renee watching her with an enigmatic smile. "What are you grinning at?" Evangeline asked, though she was fairly sure she knew precisely what was on her friend's mind.

"You sound like an old married couple, helping him like that."

Evangeline didn't bother to respond to that. Instead she lifted Ella out of her high chair and brushed the crumbs off her overalls. Then, dropping the little girl on her hip, she hooked her purse over her arm and grabbed the plates.

"Look at you, all efficient and domestic," Renee said with a laugh as she cleaned up her own plate.

"I'm a natural organizer," Evangeline said with a trace of melancholy in her voice as she clung to Ella.

Taking care of someone else's daughter…. Organizing someone else's domestic life…. Planning someone else's wedding….

Always the bridesmaid.

Don't go there, she reminded herself. *That's a dead end street.*

But even as she told herself this as she and Renee parted ways, she felt her optimism slowly wearing thin, like a shirt worn too long, the fabric barely holding together.

She looked at Ella, this precious little girl whose father barely knew her, a sense of dissatisfaction niggling at her. This little girl was worming her way into Evangeline's heart.

And her father?

Evangeline shook off the feeling and strode out of the coffee shop. The sooner Denny's sister arrived, the better it would be for everyone.

"I am so sorry about this."

Evangeline, still holding Ella in her arms, looked back at Denny from the dining room of the ranch house, her woebegone expression almost making him laugh.

Only the state of the house kept him from giving in to his mirth.

Muddy footprints encrusted the parts of the floor not covered with papers, old rags and discarded clothes. The kitchen counters were hidden by dirty dishes, pizza and take-out boxes, and paper plates encrusted with stuff Denny didn't want to inspect.

"And this is only the kitchen and dining room," Evangeline moaned, taking another turn as if trying to absorb the mess.

Denny pushed his hands through his hair as one more obstacle was dropped into his already crowded path. He had come straight here from work, his head still ringing from the constant drone of his truck, his eyes gritty with dust from the gravel pit, feeling as though he couldn't run fast enough to keep up to his life. The cows were arriving tonight.

And now this?

Some help here, Lord?

Evangeline pressed her lips together, her eyes narrowing as she looked around the room. "I should have checked on them more often," she said, anger taking over her dismay. "If I ever see them again…" She let the sentence trail off as if she understood herself the likelihood of ever running into three boys and a girl from New Zealand in Hartley Creek again.

In spite of his own frustration, Denny had to smile at her anger. "I'll just have to stay late and clean it up."

"Don't be silly," Evangeline retorted. "You don't have time. You're too busy getting everything else done. And your yearlings are coming tonight," she said.

As if on cue, Denny heard the muted roar of a truck growing louder, then the sound of it downshifting.

"They're here now."

"You go deal with your animals. Ella and I will clean up in here, won't we, Ella?" Evangeline said with a wide smile, tickling his daughter under her chin.

Denny looked from Ella to Evangeline, feeling torn as the sound of the truck grew louder. Ella was his responsibility, not Evangeline's.

"Let me take Ella," he said. "Then you can go home."

"Don't be silly. You'll have your hands full unloading those animals and making sure they don't get out of the corrals. It won't be safe for Ella anyhow."

"I guess you're right." He hesitated a moment, still feeling as if he was expecting too much from Evangeline.

Then she flapped her hand at him. "Go. Make sure those creatures are unloaded okay."

"Thanks again." He gave Evangeline and Ella a quick smile, then headed out the door just as the cattle liner pulled into the yard with a hundred head of bawling, hungry and cranky cows and yearlings.

He hurried over to the corrals. The gates to the pasture were shut and the corrals were solid. He had a tractor coming that he had rented from a local dealer and another truck arriving with hay.

An hour later the animals were unloaded, their bawling drowning out much of the conversation he'd tried to have with the trucker.

"Thanks for doing this on such short notice," Denny yelled as he scribbled out a check on the top of the nearest fence post, blinking at the dust raised by a hundred sets of hooves in the dry dirt of the corrals.

"No problem. They look like a nice bunch of animals," the trucker called back, tucking the check into the back pocket of his shiny blue jeans. He tipped a stained hat back on his head and looked over the gathered cows. "Bart had a nice herd built up. His wife was so happy you bought them."

Denny slipped the pen back into his pocket, giving the trucker a weak smile. At the last minute he had decided to purchase the majority of

Bart's herd. It had been part of Denny's long-term plan that, like everything else so far, had become part of a short-term plan. However, Bart had given him a good deal and Denny knew that once he sold the calves that came with the cows, he'd get half of his cost back. It was a good investment. A smart investment.

The timing was rotten but he couldn't let the deal slip out of his hands. More importantly, Bart had built up his cow herd using animals Denny had had to sell when he'd sold his family's ranch. By buying them back, Denny felt as if he had regained a connection to what he'd lost two years ago. A connection to the herd his own father had so painstakingly raised.

"Well, good luck with them," the trucker said, tucking a wad of chew in his mouth. He sauntered off, climbed into his truck, and with a hiss of brakes and a puff of smoke, the truck lumbered out of the yard.

Denny glanced over the herd milling around the corrals. Thankfully the waterers worked. Now he simply had to wait for the tractor to be delivered and the feed to arrive.

He felt a tense agitation at the thought of the cows and calves having to wait to be fed after their stressful trip.

One step at a time.

He turned just as Evangeline came walking

from the house toward him, holding Ella on her hip.

"Hey, everything okay?" he asked, walking toward them.

She nodded, giving him a quick smile that didn't help his resolve much. The more time he spent with this woman, the harder it became to keep aloof from her. To remind himself that he wasn't the person for her.

She looked past him to the gathered herd, still bawling, still upset. "Those calves look too young for yearlings," she said.

Denny shrugged. "I bought Bart's herd. A bit ahead of my five-year plan, but then my plan is in shreds right about now anyway."

Evangeline's expression shifted into a slow, careful smile. "Are you saying that part of your plan was to eventually have a calving operation?"

He shrugged as he brushed the dust off his shirt. "As long as I drove truck, I didn't figure I could calve out cows, but since I can't truck full-time because of Ella, I figured I may as well get a start on the herd."

"On this ranch?"

"If your dad will go through with the plan we hatched."

"Plan?"

"The lease agreement was to give me some

space. I was hoping to buy it from him after that time."

Evangeline shook her head, a mixture of emotions chasing across her face as she shifted Ella on her hip, tilting her head to one side as if studying him from another angle. "So you planned to settle down."

"Eventually."

"I see."

Her cryptic comment made him even more puzzled, and he was about to ask her what she meant when the rumble of an engine sounded above the noise of the cows.

Puzzled, he spun around in time to see a red-and-black tractor pulling into the yard with a round bale balanced on the front-end loader. It was pulling a wagon with a couple more bales teetering on it.

"What in the world—?" He frowned, completely at a loss. The tractor was to have been delivered later today.

And the hay...

"That's what I came out to tell you," Evangeline said, resting her hand on his arm to get his attention. "I called Carter Beck and told him what had happened to you. He ranches just up the valley. He's here to help."

Denny blinked the dust from his eyes as the

fist that had a permanent hold on his stomach released some of its grip.

He looked back at her, grinning like a kid. "You are amazing."

As their eyes held he felt as if her bright smile dove into his soul and settled there.

He didn't want to look away and it seemed neither did she. The bawling of the cows and the drone of the tractor bracketed them, but Denny could only think of how Evangeline's face lit up when she smiled.

Then the tractor grew louder, and the cows, as if sensing that supper was coming, increased their own bellowing.

Denny gave her a quick nod then jogged toward the tractor. A tall, dark-haired man was driving. A young boy was perched behind him in the cab, a battered and worn cowboy hat sitting on the back of his head.

"Hi, Mr. Denny," the little boy called when Carter reached down and opened the door of the cab. "We brought some food for your cows."

Denny flashed him a quick grin and a thumbs-up, then pulled himself up on the lower step of the tractor, putting him eye level with Carter.

"I can't thank you enough for this," he said over the roar of the tractor.

Carter just grinned back at him, his teeth white against the dark stubble shading his chin. "No problem. I'm guessing you want a couple of bales put out in the corrals?"

Denny explained where they should go and Carter nodded. Denny jumped off the step and ran back to the corrals. He clambered over a fence, closed one gate, opened another, and a few minutes later Carter had unhooked from the wagon and transferred the first bale into the corrals. When they were done, three bales were spread out and three more lay ready for the next time the cows needed to be fed. The bawling had quieted to an occasional bleat from a calf and the sound of a herd of cows chewing on hay.

Carter had parked the tractor, turned it off, and was talking to Evangeline when Denny joined them.

"Peace at last, eh?" Carter said, flashing Denny a grin as he tipped his cowboy hat back on his head and rested his elbows on the top rail of the fence.

"Best sound in the world," Denny returned, coming to stand beside Carter and Evangeline. The little boy was standing on the first rung of the fence, his posture a miniature replica of Carter's.

Evangeline had set Ella on the fence, wrapping her arms around the little girl to hold her steady.

"Looks like they've mothered up pretty good," Carter said. "Nice herd of cows."

"Purebred Red Angus," Denny said with a

note of pride. Watching the cows now, offspring from the animals he and his father had raised, created a connection to his father and the ranch he'd sold.

Maybe his life would work out, he thought with a lift of his heart. He looked at Ella sitting on the fence, Evangeline holding her. Ella clapped her hands and laughed as a calf skipped past them, tail up, its hide glistening in the sun.

"I think she likes them," Evangeline said, slipping Denny a quick sideways glance.

A sense of rightness settled in his restless soul as he looked at Evangeline. He took in a cleansing breath and put his elbows up on the fence, his arm brushing hers. She didn't move and together they watched the cows, sharing this moment of peace and contentment as Ella babbled her happiness.

"Well, Adam, we better get back to your mom and little sister," Carter said, pushing away from the fence. "Evangeline tells me that the fences aren't great. Zach said the same thing when he boarded his horses here, but horses are easier to keep in than cows. Me and my foreman, Wade, will come by tomorrow and help you get them ready."

"That's not necessary," Denny said automatically.

"I think it is," Carter returned with a grin.

"You might be able to get it done but it will go faster with some neighborly help."

Denny felt overwhelmed. He barely knew these people and they were already volunteering to help him out.

"I don't know what to say."

"Don't bother," Carter said, pulling his leather gloves out of his back pocket and tugging them on. Then he shot Denny another grin. "Good fences make good neighbors. If your fences don't hold, your cows will be heading over to my pasture."

Then, with another wave, Carter sauntered back to the tractor, Adam following him step for step.

As Carter started the tractor up and hooked it up to the wagon again, Denny turned to Evangeline, touching her arm to get her attention. "I know you organized this," he said. "I can't thank you enough."

She shrugged, looking down at Ella, tickling her under her chin. "Carter and Emma are good people and like to help out."

The sound of his daughter's laughter feathered through the air, light, happy and content, her chubby hands tangled in Evangeline's hair.

Evangeline winced and Denny reached over to help release them. As he did, their hands brushed each other.

Neither pulled away and as their eyes met once again Denny couldn't stop a sense of expectancy rising in his soul.

Could something be happening between them? Did he dare let it?

Chapter Eight

Evangeline glanced at the clock. Only five-thirty. She had a casserole in the oven upstairs that would be ready at six. She was taking it with her to the ranch.

Denny had been so busy fixing fences yesterday, she was sure he hadn't eaten much for supper. Today he would be driving a truck and she knew he wouldn't have time to cook. So today she made a casserole for him. Just a good neighborly thing to do. That was all.

She walked to the back of the store to see what Ella was up to. The little girl sat in the middle of the space Evangeline had cleared for her future children's corner, cuddling a teddy bear, babbling in her own high-pitched jargon. Evangeline had been taking care of her the past few days and had enjoyed every minute she spent with the little girl.

Evangeline knew she had to be careful. Every night she brought Ella back to Denny's it grew harder to leave Denny and Ella and the ranch for her quiet, lonely apartment.

Half an hour later Evangeline had locked up the store early and the casserole dish was wrapped in towels and sitting in a box beside Ella. Ella sat in the back waving her hands as she babbled and hummed along to the children's CD Evangeline had playing on her car stereo.

As Evangeline drove the road leading to the ranch, her heart lifted. She always loved going there, but when it was rented or leased out to other occupants she felt as if she were intruding when she dropped in.

But for the past couple of days she had a good reason to go, and looked forward to seeing cows on the pasture once again.

And seeing Denny?

Evangeline parked her car beside a large gravel truck and trailer. As she got out she heard Denny call her name.

And why did her heart give that silly jump at the sound of his voice as it had each time she heard it? She pulled herself together. "Hey, there," she said, opening the back door of the car and unbuckling Ella as he came around his truck.

"Good timing. I just pulled in ten minutes ago. How's my girl been today?" Denny asked, wiping his arm across his forehead, making a dirty streak on his chambray shirt.

"Great. Do you want to take her?" she asked, pulling Ella out of the car seat.

Denny looked down at his grimy hands and shook his head. "I'll stain that cute outfit."

As Evangeline set Ella on the ground, she tugged the little girl's ruffled T-shirt down over her plaid shorts. "I picked it up at Reflections today," Evangeline murmured, feeling suddenly self-conscious of her impulsive purchase. "All her other clothes were dirty."

"Of course. I'll have to figure out how to get her laundry done, too," Denny said with the faintest sigh.

"I can take care of it for now," Evangeline said, taking the box out of the backseat.

"You get Ella. I'll take that," Denny said, sniffing as he relieved Evangeline of the box. "Whatever is in here sure smells good."

"I thought you might be too busy to cook today, so I made a casserole for you and Ella," Evangeline said casually.

"Wow. You didn't have to do that." Denny gave her a crooked smile. "Not that I'm complaining."

Evangeline chuckled as she picked Ella up and followed Denny to the house.

"Has Ella eaten yet?" Denny asked.

Evangeline nodded as he held the door of the

house open for her. "I wasn't sure when I would be able to get here and I didn't want her to have to wait."

"Did you have supper yet?"

Without thinking, Evangeline shook her head.

"Then you better join me. After all, you made this."

"No. That's okay.... I've got stuff to do...."

Denny held up his hand to stop her. "Of course. I understand."

Evangeline nodded, and when she entered the kitchen she felt again a clutch of dismay as she saw the mess. Though she had stayed for a while yesterday after she dropped Ella off to help, there was still so much to do.

"Do you mind watching Ella for a few more minutes while I wash up?" he asked as he set the box on the counter.

"Of course not," Evangeline said. As Denny left, she looked around the kitchen and shook her head. She and Denny had gotten rid of the pizza boxes and take-out containers, but the counters and sink still looked grimy and the stove was a sticky disaster. She knew the rest of the house wasn't much better. She set Ella on her hip and, one-handed, filled the sink with warm water and cleanser to start cleaning the stove.

"Sorry about the mess," Denny said as he returned, his face and hands clean, his hair brushed. Stubble still shaded his chin, giving him a rugged look. "I haven't had time to clean—"

"I'm the one who should be apologizing," Evangeline protested. "I should have checked on the renters more often." Thankfully she hadn't given them their damage deposit back. She had hoped to use it to hire a cleaning service, but the only one available was in Cranbrook, and couldn't come until next week.

"At least the table and chairs are clean, thanks to your work last night," Denny said, reaching out to take Ella from her.

Evangeline looked around, once more feeling guilty over the mess. "Why don't I finish cleaning up the kitchen while you eat and feed Ella?"

"Now that's just awkward," Denny said. "Besides, it would be crazy not to eat the casserole you made. Unless it's really gross?"

Evangeline giggled and shook her head. "It's my grandmother's recipe. My favorite."

"Then, please, let's eat together."

Evangeline felt another protest spring to her lips but then she glanced his way and caught his smile and her resistance shifted. "Okay," she conceded. "But as soon as we're done I'm getting to work here."

"Deal."

Denny set a hot plate on the table and the casserole on top as Evangeline took out the paper plates, plastic utensils and napkins from the bag she brought along, and set it all on the table.

Ella banged her fists on the table, jabbering away. Denny picked her up and put her on his lap. "I'll have to get her another high chair for when she's here," he said.

"I can bring one when I come tomorrow," Evangeline replied as she sat at the table. "I'm sure I can find one in town."

She was about to dish up the food when she saw Denny take Ella's hands and put them together. "Now, Ella, we're going to pray for this amazing food that Evangeline brought us," he said, bending his head over her, his dark hair a contrast to her blond curls.

Evangeline folded her hands, as well, as Denny angled her a smile. Then he bowed his head.

"Dear Lord," he prayed. "Thank You for this wonderful food. Thank You for the hands that prepared them. Help us to trust in You always and in everything. And thank You that Your love is never-ending and that You always find us. Amen."

She clenched her hands together as his simple and sincere prayer soothed her thirsty soul.

But even more, it created a gentle yearning for Denny's basic faith.

She lifted her head to see him looking down at Ella, smiling. "Say 'amen,' sweetie," he urged.

The endearment came naturally. For a man who didn't know this little girl even existed a week ago, he was doing remarkably well at connecting with her. A wave of envy flowed through Evangeline as she wondered why her father—who had seen her born, had helped her through the first eight years of her life—had acted so differently.

"Say 'amen,'" Denny prompted again.

"Ahh, ahh" was Ella's burbling reply.

"Good girl," Denny said, giving her a quick hug. "She's a smart little thing," Denny said, a tinge of pride in his voice. "Say Dada," he prompted.

Ella clapped her hands and laughed. "Mama. Mama. Mama."

The spoon Evangeline was holding clattered onto the table. She shot Denny a horrified look, suddenly self-conscious. "I don't know where she got that from," she blurted. She hoped he didn't think she had taught Ella that.

"Don't apologize. I'm sure she called Lila that," he said, giving her a quick smile as Evangeline picked up the spoon and served him his casserole. "And this looks and smells amazing. I'm starving."

"Do you want me to take Ella so you can eat?" she offered.

He shook his head, his fork in one hand, his

other holding Ella. "I don't mind. I haven't seen her all day."

Evangeline nodded, served herself, and as soon as she started eating, so did Denny.

Neither spoke as they ate and Evangeline kept her attention on the food on her plate. Finally she looked across the table and was disconcerted to catch Denny looking at her. She ducked her head, wishing she had simply gone straight home instead of offering to help him clean the house.

"So, tell me, how did your dad get this ranch?" Denny asked, breaking the silence.

Evangeline wiped her mouth and gave him a quick smile. "He took it over from his father shortly after he and my mother married. His father wanted to get out of the business. He lives in Kelowna now."

"It's a good-size spread," Denny said. "And the bookstore?"

"My grandparents—my mother's parents— owned it, but they died a couple of years after my mom got married. Her sister, my aunt Josie, managed it for my father after my mother…after she died."

Denny shifted Ella on his lap as she reached out for his plate. "That must have been a hard time for you," he said quietly.

Evangeline too easily recalled that bleak, empty part of her life. "It was difficult," she said carefully, aware of Denny's friendship with her father.

She didn't want to mention that time was doubly difficult because her father hadn't stayed around, either. When he'd dropped her off at the bookstore, Evangeline had felt as if she had lost two parents instead of one.

"I'm sure you know how hard that must be," she said, turning the conversation back to him. "After your parents died."

"It was hard. But I learned I had to trust God and I know He pulled me through."

"You have a strong faith in God, don't you?"

"You sound surprised."

"Not surprised. Maybe a little envious."

"Why would you be envious?"

Evangeline shrugged, not sure what to say. She didn't talk about her faith much. Never had with her father or Tyler.

And maybe that was part of the problem with those relationships, she thought.

"You believe in God, don't you?" he asked, his quiet question digging up old memories of church, of reading her Bible, of a relationship that had, at one time, been the most important in her life.

And the only stable one.

"I do. I always have. I've just…neglected my faith for a while."

"Can I ask why?"

Evangeline shrugged. "It's not out of bitterness, if that's what you're thinking. Just…neglect. Got caught up with a boyfriend who never went to church. After we broke up I got busy with the store, trying to find a way to make it profitable. Trying to put my own stamp on it. God kind of took a backseat to all of that."

"Do you miss God?"

His question laid bare the emptiness of her life the past few years. An emptiness she had never wanted to examine too deeply because she knew it would mean refocusing her life and changing her priorities.

Then she released a light laugh, devoid of humor. "Actually, I do."

"So why don't you go to church?"

"Seems strange to me now. To go after all this time."

"You know the story of the prodigal son."

"Of course."

"I always found it interesting that when the son returned, the father immediately ran toward him because he was waiting for his son's return." Denny gave her a quick smile. "I like to think that every day the father would get up, go to the road and wait. That's the picture Jesus gave us of God."

"I've always had trouble with the image of

God as Father," she said quietly, pushing some rice around her plate, avoiding Denny's sincere gaze. "In my story I was the one who waited, not my father. And it seems I'm still waiting." That last comment came out with a bitter note that she immediately regretted. She was telling him things she had only ever told Renee, her best and dearest friend.

And Denny was her father's friend and had probably heard her father's version of his story.

"Your father has often said that being in Hartley Creek was hard for him," Denny said. "After losing his wife."

His defense of her father was admirable but Evangeline felt a flicker of anger.

"He was miserable after my mother died" was her careful reply. "He left me alone a lot."

"I thought he spent a lot of time with you?"

She wished she hadn't let the words spill out, but somehow being around him lowered her defenses. She wasn't saying anything more, but then his eyes met hers and in their dark depths she saw sympathy.

And his questions and attentiveness slowly drew out the memories.

"When my mother died, my father was devastated. I know that. I know he loved her. So did I. But a month after her funeral he dropped me off at my aunt's place. Aunt Josie had helped my mother run the bookstore. She lived in my grand-parents' old apartment above it. Andy asked if she could take care of me. I remember crying when he left. I was still dealing with the loss of my mother and a month later my father left me."

Denny shook his head. "How long was he gone?"

"About six months. When he came back I thought we were moving back onto the ranch. Instead he fixed up the apartment you were staying in. We lived there whenever he came home. He was around a couple of months and then gone again." She stopped, aware of the sour note entering her voice. "But that was a long time ago."

"Maybe, but it must have been hard. Being abandoned when you had your own grief to deal with," he said. "What was your aunt like?"

Evangeline gave him a careful shrug. "I think she tried her best. She was a single woman who had never had children of her own. I don't think she knew what to do with me half of the time. I spent a lot of time in the bookstore. It became my refuge, my one connection to my mother."

"That's sad." Then, to her surprise, he reached over and laid his hand on her arm in sympathy.

His hand was warm and rough. The hands of a working man.

And his light caress sent a tingle up her spine. She should pull her arm away, but didn't want to. It had been a long time since someone other than her friends had expressed concern for her.

And a long time since the touch of a man had created this kind of reaction.

Her practical mind told her he was only being sympathetic. However, as she looked into his eyes it was more than sympathy she saw glinting in their brown depths.

"It was hard," she said. "But eventually I got accustomed to my dad's comings and goings and promises that someday we'd move back onto the ranch and have a normal life. Obviously that never happened. Thankfully I had the bookstore to keep me focused and busy." She pressed her lips against the spill of words. Goodness, she was getting maudlin. She had to stop before she started feeling even sorrier for herself.

"Still, I'm sorry you had to deal with that." He finally pulled his hand away and she felt a sense of loss.

She gave him a regretful smile, covering up her reaction to his touch. "You don't have to apologize for that."

"Sorry. Force of habit from living with three sisters," he said with a quick grin.

"How so?"

"Even if whatever happened wasn't my fault— the lost book, the boyfriend who didn't like them, the girlfriend who was fighting with them—my sisters would often find a way to make it my problem. So Nate and I learned early on to live in a state of abject apology."

Evangeline laughed at that, thankful for his easy return to a lighter subject. "Nate being your foster brother?"

"Yeah."

"How long did he stay with you?"

"He came when he was twelve. Tough, angry kid, but he mellowed. My parents loved him and my sisters teased him and he followed me around everywhere. It was hard on him when my parents died."

"I'm surprised social services let him stay with you after that."

Denny pulled Ella's hand away from his plate. "He was sixteen at the time. At that age he could have moved out on his own. He chose to stay at the ranch until…" He let the sentence fade away.

"Until…?" Evangeline prompted.

"Until Lila and I got divorced." Denny scooped up a small amount of the casserole onto his fork and lifted it to Ella's lips. "You want to try some of this, baby girl?"

But Ella batted her hand at the fork, spilling the food.

"Sorry," Denny said, wiping it up with his hand as he gave Evangeline a sheepish grin.

"That can be cleaned," Evangeline said, pushing herself away from the table to get some napkins, sensing Denny didn't want to talk about Lila.

And she didn't dare question him the way he had questioned her about her faith.

Partly because she didn't want to know about Lila. Didn't want to know how deeply Denny grieved her death.

And why not? Is it because you might be envious?

She brushed that question aside, but when she returned to the table he looked up. When their eyes met, her heart shifted.

She wiped at the chicken and rice, then, picking up the casserole dish, as well, turned away, her heart battling with her mind. He had no room for her in his life and she didn't want to be a part of it. She had chosen wrong before, put her trust in the wrong person. She didn't dare repeat that mistake.

But even as her heart and mind did battle, her resolve shifted.

He is a man of faith. A man of integrity.

A man who had a baby to take care of and an ex-wife to grieve, the practical part of her mind told her.

"Oh, I almost forgot to tell you," Denny said as she threw the napkin into the garbage. "My sister is finally coming to the ranch on Monday to help me out with Ella."

"So you won't need me anymore?" She kept her back turned to him, surprised his news created this bloom of desolation.

"Probably not."

Evangeline nodded, fussing with the casserole dish, scraping the leftovers into a container she had brought along for that express purpose. "That's good," she said, forcing a cheerful note to her voice. "That will work out great." She glanced through the window over the kitchen sink, looking out at the ranch. If his sister came, she wouldn't need to come out here anymore.

She closed her eyes. This was good. This was the way it should be. She was becoming too attached to Ella.

Too attached to Denny.

"I want you to know how much I appreciate your help," Denny continued as she fussed unnecessarily with the container, making sure she got the lid on exactly right.

"No problem," she replied. "Gladly done." But she still couldn't turn to face him. "I'll just put this in the fridge and then I'll be on my way," she murmured.

"You don't have to leave yet," he said.

Oh, yes, I do, she thought. The situation was getting complicated. And she was getting too attached.

It was a good thing his sister was coming, she

thought fifteen minutes later as she drove off the ranch.

The best thing that could happen.

So why did she feel an emptiness growing in her heart as each passing moment took her farther from the ranch?

"Seriously, Olivia?" Denny tucked his phone under his chin as he unbuckled Ella from her car seat. It was Sunday morning and he had come to church early. He was looking forward to the service. Then his sister called, effectively ruining his Sunday peace. "You promised you would come and I need you."

"Sorry. I know I said that," Olivia said. "But when I told my boss I was quitting, he said he'd give me a bonus if I stuck around another week, and you know I can use the money."

Denny pulled Ella out of the backseat of his truck and kicked the door shut. He wanted to remind Olivia of the times he'd helped her but knew that could awaken a more painful subject.

Because of his poor choice, Olivia had had to move from her home.

"I thought you had some lady helping you out," Olivia said.

"I can't keep asking her to come. She has her own business to run." And he knew that in spite of the havoc and turmoil in his own life, he was growing too attached to Evangeline. That moment in his kitchen when he had impulsively reached out and touched her had lingered long after she'd left. He couldn't afford to be distracted.

Carrying Ella, he walked around to the other side of the truck and pulled out the diaper bag Evangeline had readied for him yesterday when she'd brought Ella to the ranch. Last week he'd come to church completely unprepared. This week he didn't want to look like a poor father.

"I'll come as soon as I'm done with this job," Olivia promised. "Next week."

He'd simply have to be satisfied with that. "I'll see you by the end of next week, Livvy," he warned her.

"Looking forward to meeting my little niece."

"I hope so." He was nearing the front doors of the church. "I gotta go. Send me a text when you know when you're coming."

"Roger that." She signed off, leaving Denny in the lurch once again.

Denny sighed, turned his phone to silent and slipped it into his shirt pocket. Sisters. Never there when he needed them, only there when they wanted something from him. Now he would have to ask Evangeline to continue to help him.

That thought frightened him and sent anticipation singing through him at the same time. As he pulled open the door of the church the aroma of fresh-brewed coffee assaulted his nostrils. He'd missed his morning coffee and his breakfast.

While he'd fed Ella he'd been on the phone going over final details with Carlos, then arranging for more feed for the cows. Taking care of everyone but himself.

And trying not to remember Evangeline sitting across from him last night as she ate supper with him as if it was the most normal thing in the world.

As she listened to him talk about his faith. After she'd left he'd felt as if he had come on a bit strong. He'd only wanted her to know that God cared for her.

Because you're starting to care about her.

It was as if the boundaries he had placed around his heart were slowly being erased by Evangeline's continued presence.

"Hey, Denny, good to see you." Carter Beck stopped to say hi, waggling his fingers at Ella. "And you, little girl. You're a cute one."

"That she is," Denny agreed, the diaper bag starting to dig into his shoulder. What had Evangeline put in the thing? An iron to smooth out any wrinkles in Ella's clothes?

"If you need a place to sit, you can join us," Carter said. "I know how hard it can be to come to a new church."

"Sure. Thanks," Denny returned. "I'll just take Ella to the nursery."

"You know where it is?"

"Someone showed me last week," he said. He turned to walk down the hall and then, suddenly, Ella clapped her hands.

"Mama. Mama," she called out, netting a few smiles from some of the other people gathered in the foyer.

Denny looked up and there was Evangeline.

She wore the same white-and-gold dress she'd worn to show him around the ranch. A flower clip held her hair to one side, letting the rest wave over her shoulder.

Cute as a button. Pretty as a picture.

The clichéd words sprang unbidden to his mind and Denny felt his cheeks warm as their eyes met. Then she smiled.

"Mama. Mama," Ella repeated, leaning away from him, making him lose his balance.

Evangeline hurried over to his side and took Ella from him, shushing her, her cheeks even redder than Denny's felt. "Sorry about that," she muttered, pressing one perfectly manicured finger to Ella's lips. "Shh, honey," she whispered.

Ella giggled, reaching for the flower in Evangeline's hair.

"Good to see you here" was all Denny could say.

Evangeline gave him a shy smile. "I couldn't

stop thinking about what you said. So I thought I would come back."

And why did that create this surge of well-being?

"I better let you take her," Evangeline said.

"Why don't you come with me?" Denny blurted out, holding up the bag she had put together. "Maybe you can explain to the attendants what all's in this thing? I didn't have time to look through it."

She chuckled and as they walked to the church nursery he let his lonely, foolish heart imagine they were a family.

But no sooner had that thought formulated than he shook it off. He couldn't afford to go there. He had too many obligations and too little to give her.

Evangeline handed Ella to the attendant while Denny filled out the instruction sheet and took a number that corresponded to the number clipped to Ella's shirt.

As the young girl walked away with Ella, his daughter looked over the girl's shoulder and her lip began to quiver. She held out one arm to him and Denny hesitated.

"We should go before she starts crying," Evangeline warned, placing her hand on his arm and applying a gentle pressure.

Denny nodded. In spite of feeling as though

he was abandoning Ella, he was far too aware of Evangeline's hand, warm on his arm.

They walked together back to the foyer and through the double doors into the sanctuary. The usher smiled at them, then beckoned for them to follow him.

Denny was about to correct his assumption that they were together but then he glanced at Evangeline. She shrugged, then followed the young man to the seat he had found for them.

Denny took the bulletin from the well-meaning usher and slipped onto the pew, beside Evangeline. He nodded at Carter, who was one pew up and across the aisle from him, then ducked his head and pretended to read the paper he clutched. A few minutes later the service began and filled the awkward silence.

But the whole time he sat there he was completely aware of Evangeline. For a moment he regretted encouraging her to come back to church.

Because during the service she was a complete distraction to him. And while he was happy she had come, he wasn't sure what to do about his reaction to her.

Chapter Nine

Evangeline clung to the pew in front of her, her head bowed as the pastor pronounced the benediction.

"The Lord bless you and keep you. The Lord make His face shine upon you, and be gracious to you. The Lord turn His face toward you and give you peace."

Evangeline let the words from Numbers soak into her soul like water on parched and thirsty ground.

She looked sidelong at Denny, thankful he had encouraged her to come.

He turned at that moment and gave her a smile that made her suddenly blush. This was getting out of hand, she thought, turning away. Last night, as she'd lain in bed, he was all she could think about.

During the service, her attention was divided

between the pastor's message and Denny's presence beside her. Every time he shifted and his shoulder brushed hers, she felt a trembling awareness.

Thank goodness his sister was coming tomorrow. She could get back to her life.

What life? Working in a store that doesn't belong to you? Waiting for Prince Charming to come swooping into the store to rescue you?

She dismissed the snide thoughts that rang too close to the truth as she forced herself to turn away from Denny. Church was over. Time to leave.

But just as she was about to exit the pew, he touched her shoulder, catching her attention. She turned, her heart leaping in her chest.

"I just got a call from Olivia," Denny said, looking apologetic. "She can't come tomorrow."

"Oh. I see." Evangeline blinked as the implications of what he was saying settled in.

"I hate to ask—"

"You need help with Ella," Evangeline finished for him, surprised at the rush of joy his news gave her.

"I'm sorry—"

She held her hand up to stop him. "I don't mind. I've gotten used to having that little munchkin in my store. She's good for business."

Denny looked so relieved, Evangeline had to resist the urge to pat his shoulder.

"I'm easing Carlos into the managing of the trucks," he said. "So, eventually I'll have more time, but for now I could use the help. I know I'm asking a lot."

She gave him a quick smile, relief and a curious mixture of anticipation singing through her.

She could still see Ella.

And Denny.

"I told you I don't mind. Stop apologizing."

He gave her a grin and then stepped aside so she could walk out. As she met his eyes, her heart trembled in her chest.

Be careful, she warned herself.

But as they walked out of the church side by side she felt as if she was in exactly the right place.

•

"Did you run all the way here from wherever you were?" Mia asked as Evangeline let her, Renee and Sophie into the bookstore. "You look glowing."

It was book club night and Evangeline *was* running late. She had taken Ella to the ranch precisely at six—just as Denny had pulled up in his truck. He'd looked so weary and tired she had helped him feed Ella and then lingered to heat up the supper she had brought for him and to talk.

It was the talking that had put her behind schedule. But it was also the talking that had put a flush on her cheeks. She hadn't meant for the conversation to go so long but she'd wanted to thank him for encouraging her to go to church, and one topic of conversation had led to another.

"Sorry I'm late," she said as she walked ahead of the group to the back room. A few toys still lay on the floor, left over from Ella's wanderings around the store this afternoon. She dropped them into a basket tucked in one corner of the room.

"You still taking care of that little girl?" Mia asked as she set a tray of cookies and bars she had made on the table by the coffee urn. "I thought you were done last week."

"His sister was supposed to come but she ditched him last minute."

"And you offered to help poor Denny out. How sweet. How unselfish. How romantic."

Evangeline chose to ignore Mia's teasing comment. "Do you mind filling up the coffee urn?" she asked Renee.

"I will gladly help out my busy, busy friend," Renee said, giving her friend a knowing look.

It was going to be a long book club meeting.

Angie came later, Jeff walking alongside, teasing her. Angie would only give him a vague nod in response, and Evangeline felt sorry for the guy. He seemed pretty crazy about Angie but she seemed oblivious to his attention. Evangeline wondered if she looked the same way when talking to Denny.

But while Angie seemed unaware of Jeff, Evangeline vividly remembered how Denny smiled at her, held her eyes. How his face had lit up when he'd seen her getting out of her car.

Evangeline tried not to think about Denny. However, now and again, as Angie and Jeff went head-to-head about a part of the book they disagreed on, her mind wandered off to a ranch and a house with a little girl and a man with coffee-brown eyes.

Denny glanced at the clock on the dash of his truck. Half an hour late. Again. He downshifted as he turned down the road running alongside the fields of the ranch. Brown cows dotted the green pasture, carpeting the hills, their calves racing around, tails up, enjoying the waning warmth of the day.

The sight made him smile but what really put a grin on his lips was coming around the corner and seeing a familiar little silver car pulled up beside the house.

Evangeline was waiting.

It was that thought that made him hurry, hit the brakes, park and jump out of his truck. He jogged up the walkway. Once inside the house he toed off his boots and declared, "Hey, Evangeline. I'm home."

All he heard was the sound of Ella crying. He followed it to the living room, where Evangeline sat in one of the recliners they had moved from her father's apartment to the house.

She was holding Ella, who lay against her chest, crying, her cheeks red, her curls damp.

Evangeline looked up when Denny entered the living room, then struggled to stand.

"Just stay there," he said, motioning for her to stay down. He perched on the edge of the love seat across from her. He finger-combed his hair, suddenly aware of his grimy pants and shirt, and pulled his hand over his stubbled chin. He must look a mess. "What's wrong with Ella?"

"She's running a fever," Evangeline said, stroking Ella's rosy cheeks. "Mia gave me some children's medication to bring it down, but it isn't helping much."

"Should we take her to the hospital?"

"Mia thought it might be teeth," Evangeline said, giving him a reassuring look. "Ella's cheeks are red and she's been digging at her ears. According to Mia, both are sure signs of teeth coming through."

"You're sure about that?" he said, his sudden anxiety easing.

"I'm no mother, but I'll go with what Mia told me. She does have four kids, after all."

"That's a lot of responsibility. I figure one is more than enough," he said, blowing out a relieved breath. He got up and crouched beside Evangeline, laying his hand on Ella's head. She was burning up. "Poor kid. Are you sure there's not anything else we can do?"

Evangeline shook her head, keeping her eyes lowered.

Denny looked from Ella to Evangeline, a surprising feeling of rightness washing over him. For the past week he had arrived home at the same time Evangeline had. She would bring Ella into the house and get her ready for bed while Denny washed up. They would spend a few moments talking together as Evangeline told him what Ella did that day.

And each evening when she drove off the yard he felt a sense of loss. He couldn't expect her to stay, but after that evening, when they'd shared a meal, loneliness gripped him each time she left.

Now she was still here, holding his little girl. And when she looked over at him, their eyes locking, he felt a pang of expectation. Of hovering on the edge of an uncharted path.

He only knew that for the first time in a long time he wanted to take that next step.

"Why don't you clean up and I can give her to

you," Evangeline said, her practical voice breaking into his daydream.

"Okay. Sure." He pushed himself to his feet and strode to the bathroom.

He washed his hands and face, and as the greasy dust swirled down the drain he looked at his reflection in the mirror. A rough-looking character stared back.

Who did he think he was kidding, letting thoughts of Evangeline and him even enter his mind? His life was a mishmash of half-baked schemes and plans complicated by Ella. Even if Olivia came to take care of her, it would only be temporary. What could he offer someone like Evangeline? Someone who, Andy had always told him, was looking for a hero.

Well, that wasn't him. He grabbed a towel and wiped his face, then with a quick breath, turned and walked back to the living room.

Ella was still crying, Evangeline still holding her. Denny reached for Ella. "You probably want to get back home."

"I suppose I should," Evangeline said. "Though the place always seems pretty quiet without Ella."

The wistful tone in her voice launched the cautious dreams of only a few moments ago.

"I imagine you're getting attached to her," Denny said as Evangeline got up out of the chair.

"When is your sister coming?" she asked, prying Ella's one arm from around her neck.

"She claims the end of this week. I'm sorry about all this."

Evangeline gave him a careful smile. "It's okay. I really don't mind." She tried to hand Ella to Denny, but the little girl's whimpers grew into sobs.

"No. No. Mama." She clung to Evangeline.

Evangeline lifted one eyebrow. "And that's probably another reason your sister should come."

Denny was about to apologize again but caught himself. There was nothing he could do about what was happening. Evangeline had volunteered to help him. And he was glad she had.

For many reasons.

But he still tried to take Ella from her.

Her sobs escalated to shrieks.

"Why don't you eat some supper," Evangeline said. "I got some soup and pasta for you from Mug Shots. It's in the kitchen."

"What about you?"

"I ate some of it while I was waiting." She held her hand up. "And don't even think about apologizing."

Denny hesitated but Evangeline waved her hand in a shooing motion. With a grin her way, he went to the kitchen and found the food she was talking about. Borscht with a chicken and provolone pasta dish. The soup was still warm. He left the soup in the plastic container, put the pasta on a plate and took everything into the living room.

He sat on the love seat and made quick work of his supper, listening as Ella's cries rose and fell. His heart broke for her.

"I think her fever is going down," Evangeline said, laying her hand on Ella's forehead. "She's not as hot as she was."

Denny wiped his mouth, balled up the napkin and shoved it into the soup container. "I'll take this away, then I can take her."

When he came back Ella was still clinging to Evangeline's neck, but this time Denny managed to pry her loose.

"Mama, Mama," she cried.

"It's okay, honey," Denny said. "Daddy's here."

"Daddy." She hiccupped.

Denny's mouth fell open and he shot Evangeline a shocked look. "Did you hear that? She said 'Daddy.'"

"That's so precious."

"Say Daddy," Denny coached, holding his daughter on his knees, facing him.

But Ella turned to find Evangeline and as soon as she saw her, reached out again.

"You have to stay with Daddy," Denny said, leaning back on the love seat, holding her squirming body as Evangeline got to her feet.

She shook out her full skirt and brushed a few crumbs from the front of her white T-shirt. Her hair looked untidy. Her T-shirt had a streak across the stomach and her cheek held a red scratch.

And she still looked fantastic.

Denny turned his attention back to Ella, who was crying again, big, fat tears streaming down her red cheeks. "Come on, baby, don't cry. What shall I do for you?"

"I packed a few of her favorite books in her bag," Evangeline said, grabbing the diaper bag sitting on the floor beside the love seat and pulling out a couple of brightly colored books. Evangeline set them beside him and took a step back, as if getting ready to leave. "She likes these. I was reading them to her this afternoon."

Denny chewed at his lip as he looked from Ella to the brightly illustrated books sitting beside him, suddenly embarrassed to admit the truth to her.

"What's wrong?" Evangeline asked.

"See. Here's the deal. I don't read." He cuddled Ella closer, then got up, rocking her while he walked.

"Okay. Maybe not for yourself, but it's for her."

Denny shook his head as he walked around the living room. "No. You didn't understand me. I don't read. At all. Can't."

This netted him another frown that made him feel even more embarrassed.

"You're dyslexic?"

"That's what I've been told."

"But you run a successful business."

If you wanted to call it that. "I find ways to work around it. I'm not completely illiterate, but it's a lot of work for me to decipher contracts and paperwork." He looked down at Ella, whose cries hadn't stilled, her body shaking with sobs. "I could try to read to her, but I don't think she'd appreciate my stumbling efforts."

"Do you want me to?" Evangeline offered.

If it meant she would stay around longer, yes. "If you think it will settle her down…"

"I think it will."

Evangeline picked up the books and sat on the love seat, motioning Denny to sit beside her. "Swap you Ella for the books," she said.

She reached for Ella, who almost jumped into Evangeline's arms, as Denny took the books off her lap.

"Okay, muffin," Evangeline said in a soothing voice, settling back, her arm now pressed against Denny's.

He wondered if he should get up, then decided he liked where he was sitting just fine.

Evangeline turned Ella around in her arms then took one of the books from Denny.

As soon as Ella saw the book she stopped crying and shoved her thumb into her mouth.

"'Bert's hat is blue,'" Evangeline read, turning the first page of the book. "'Donny's hat is red. Billy's is a pretty green and he wears it on his head.'"

Denny's eyes shifted from Ella to Evangeline, her head bent over Ella's head, her hair shimmering in the overhead light. He eased out a gentle sigh. It seemed the most natural thing in the world to slip his arm, now squashed between them, to across the back of the love seat.

Evangeline's only response was a shy smile that encouraged him to lower his arm, to curl his hand around her shoulder. Ella's fingers fluttered up and wound around his. Evangeline continued to read, her melodious voice rising and falling, filling the silence of the house.

This felt so right, Denny thought, his palm on Evangeline's shoulder, his fingers entwined with Ella's. He had a peculiar sense that for the first time in years, even after he and Lila were married, he was now home.

As Evangeline read, Ella's head drooped farther down. Her fingers loosened their grip on his hand and her breathing became even and deep.

"I think she's asleep," Denny whispered.

Evangeline set the book aside, but she didn't move and neither did Denny.

"So how was work today?" she asked.

Her question threw him but he didn't mind the idea of sitting and talking to her while Ella slept on her lap.

"Good. I think I've finally talked Carlos into managing the business for me, and I've found a part-time truck driver, which means I'll be able to spend more time on the ranch and more time taking care of Ella. I'll still have to drive at times, but not near as much as I have been."

"You won't make as much, then, will you?"

He shook his head. "No. But Ella is my priority now."

She gave him a strange smile. "You're a good man."

Her words surprised him but also created a coil of warmth deep in his soul.

"Thanks" was all he could say.

Then Evangeline smiled, her eyes shining in the light of the single lamp beside them. She didn't say anything. Didn't have to. Her look was as real as a touch and Denny's heart slowly turned over.

It was as if everything that had happened between them—the quick looks, the hesitant touches, the careful smiles—all came together in this moment.

Without stopping to second guess or to apologize, he touched his lips gently to hers and she responded.

He pulled back, his forehead resting against hers, her beautiful face a soft blur. She stroked his cheek once more, her soft fingers rasping over the stubble on his face.

"I should have shaved," he murmured, aware of how rough he looked.

"No. I like you like this," she said.

"You're an amazing woman," he replied.

She released a light chuckle and Ella stirred on her lap.

"I should put her to bed," he said.

"Probably" was Evangeline's careful reply.

With great reluctance Denny got to his feet and carefully took Ella out of Evangeline's arms.

The little girl stirred as he walked to her bedroom, but when he laid her gently down in her crib, she shifted to her side, her thumb back in her mouth. He laid a blanket over top of her, tucked her stuffed animal under her arm and hurried back to the living room.

His heart lifted when he saw Evangeline still sitting on the love seat and he took this as a silent invitation to join her.

It seemed the most natural thing to simply drop onto the seat beside her, to lay his arm across her shoulders and to pull her close to him.

She laid her head on his shoulder and took his hand in hers. She traced the scars on his fingers as if trying to read them.

"What's this one from?" she asked, her delicate finger touching a long, jagged mark on his right forearm.

He released a light laugh as the memory returned. "My sisters and I were playing tag in the barn. It was getting dark and Adrianna had covered one of the holes in the loft of the barn with straw. I saw her slip behind a bale across the loft and ran over to tag her, hit the hole and fell through. A nail was poking out of the side of the hole and I caught my arm on that."

"Ooh. Painful."

"Not as painful as my parents' reaction when they found out what she'd done." He laughed. "She was a pistol. Still is."

"She's the one hiking in Nepal?"

Denny nodded.

"Does she work?"

"Only as much as she needs to." He caught her hand in his, curving his fingers around hers. "I don't want to talk about my goofy sisters," he said. "I prefer to talk about you. I want to find out more about you."

Evangeline looked away and shrugged. "I've told you everything. My history. Nothing fascinating."

"I don't agree," he said, still trying to absorb the fact that he and Evangeline were sitting side by side on a love seat after sharing a kiss. "You fascinate me."

She turned her head and gave him a bemused look. "No one's ever said that to me before."

"Maybe no one's seen you the way I see you."

The words slipped out of him and part of his mind warned him to be cautious, warned him this was too good to be true. But the part of his heart that had always sought someone like Evangeline told him to take a chance.

Her smile caught his breath and as she leaned toward him it seemed the most natural thing in the world to meet her partway.

To kiss her again.

To ignore the voices clamoring in his head, warning him that he couldn't afford to do this. He had no space in his life for her.

"Should we be doing this?" Evangeline whispered, giving voice to his concerns.

Denny resisted the urge to apologize for something he didn't feel the least sorry about. "Are you thinking about Ella?"

"A bit," she whispered. But she leaned forward and brushed her lips across his, contradicting herself.

"I think about her, too," he said, pulling back so he could look into her eyes and read her expression.

The smile on her face quieted worries that he had overstepped a boundary.

Yet talking about Ella brought her back into the room, so to speak.

And, in spite of how his heart soared when he kissed Evangeline, Denny knew he couldn't think only of himself this time. He had Ella to consider.

"We'll take this one step at a time," he promised her.

"That's probably wise," she said, pulling back, as well.

But as she slipped out of his embrace his regret made him feel anything but wise.

Chapter Ten

Evangeline felt a lift of her heart as she parked her car beside Denny's truck parked by the ranch house.

"Hey, sweetie," she said to Ella sitting in the backseat as she turned off the engine. "Daddy's home already."

"Daddy. Daddy," Ella called, clapping her hands in glee.

Evangeline laughed at Ella's exuberance. "I know how you feel," she said as she got out then unbuckled the little girl.

Since Wednesday, when she and Denny had shared that fateful kiss, they'd both held to an unspoken agreement to keep their distance. Denny would drop Ella off as usual. Evangeline would bring her home. As usual.

However, every minute Evangeline spent with Denny, each look they exchanged, each laugh they shared, lowered the guard around her heart.

And every time she drove away from the ranch to return to her quiet and empty apartment, she felt as if she'd left something important behind.

For the first time since Tyler, she dared veer into territory she had declared off limits. A place where she dared to think about a future. Dared to think of a home. A man beside her who now had a name and a face and who was, day by day, stealing her heart.

While she was glad they were being cautious, each moment she spent with him made her more certain she could entrust her heart to this man.

"Hey, I thought I heard that fancy little car driving up."

Evangeline turned just as Denny strode across the yard toward them. He was wiping his hands on a rag, his shirtsleeves rolled up, his cowboy hat askew and his pants streaked with grease.

He looked great.

"I came early today," she said, giving him a quick smile. "I thought I could finish cleaning up that last bedroom."

"You've worked hard enough on the house." Denny took Ella from her and gave her a languid smile. "Besides, once you said you were staying for supper, I made plans for the evening."

"That sounds nefarious."

"Whatever that means," he said with a shrug. "Wicked or criminal."

"Nothing that ambitious," Denny said, reaching for the bag that held the pot of chili. "Do you want me to take that?"

"I'm good," she said, slipping the bag over her arm as she pulled out the other bag holding the cheese buns. "So tell me about your big plans for the night."

"My plans. Let's see. Supper. Then put this little one in the bathtub," he said, tapping Ella's snub nose with his finger. "Put her to bed, put our feet up and watch a movie I rented."

Evangeline grinned. "It's been a while since I've seen a movie. Which one did you get?"

"I thought I'd go traditional with *Casablanca,* but the guy doesn't get the girl at the end."

"Victor does."

"Yeah, but he's not who I was cheering for. So I went with another oldie but goodie, *The Three Stooges Hit Manhattan.*"

"What?"

Denny winked at her. "Kidding. I got *While You Were Sleeping.*"

"I love that movie." Anticipation curled through her. A movie would mean sitting beside each other all cozy.

"I can get some cleaning done before supper,

though," Evangeline said. "The mess in that room bothers me."

"Why? You don't have to stay in it."

Evangeline gave him a careful smile. "That was my bedroom."

"I should have known," Denny said. "Princess wallpaper."

Evangeline shrugged. "I liked it."

"And so you got it."

"What can I say? I was an only child and my parents loved me."

Denny just laughed, then his expression grew more serious. "Your father still loves you, you realize."

"I guess. In his own strange way."

"If the gifts he gives you are anything to go by, he cares about you a lot."

Evangeline fingered the pearl necklace she wore today. Her father had given it to her the last time he had come home. Right after he'd handed her a new digital camera. She knew he was trying to make up for his absence, but she often wished he would come empty-handed and stay longer instead of dropping into her life, throwing expensive gifts around and leaving as soon as the paper wrapping them was thrown away.

She was about to respond to Denny's comment when his phone buzzed. He pulled it out of his pocket and was soon deep in conversation with Carlos about one of the trucks.

His conversation made her heart fall. She felt a sense of déjà vu as Denny discussed the problem. Would he have to leave like her father always did?

"Doesn't matter if it won't be running. Just get a mechanic to come out and look at it," Denny said as he shouldered the door open and held it so Evangeline could come inside. "I've got plans for the night."

He gave her another wink and Evangeline's worries slipped away, followed by a quiver of anticipation and thankfulness.

She set the container holding the chili on the counter. The house looked so much better than when she'd first showed it to Denny. The countertops gleamed, the floors shone and the taps glistened.

Denny set Ella down, finished his phone call and then slipped his phone into his pocket.

"Are you okay here?" he asked. "After I get the work done on the fence, I can come back."

"You go do your ranch stuff and I'll get at that room."

"I told you to leave it be."

She shook her head, putting him off with a smile. He paused a moment then ran one finger down her cheek, his eyes holding a gentle warmth and the hint of a promise. Her heart vaulted against her chest, her breath lost in her throat, and for an electrifying moment she thought he would kiss her again.

But he just gave her a smile, then, whistling a jaunty tune, sauntered out of the house, leaving Evangeline to speculate and hope.

"Good night, sleep tight," Denny whispered, stroking Ella's cheek. She looked up at him, her lower lip quivering in the dim glow cast by the night-light.

"It's okay, honey," he said, stroking her back. "Just go to sleep. Normally I'd love to sit and chat with you," he said, keeping his voice quiet and soothing. "But Daddy has other plans. So you have to help him out and go to sleep. And if things go well, maybe there will be some changes around here."

He caught himself with a wry laugh. Ella's presence in his life was the biggest change.

But the change he was thinking of could fit so well with Ella's sudden appearance. Could be what he'd been seeking since he was a young man, wanting to find the right person to share his life with.

For a moment a sense of unease shivered down his neck. He had thought Ella's mother was that person. But he shook that thought off. His and

Lila's relationship had had a rocky start and she had taken advantage of him.

Evangeline was so different.

"So go to sleep, little girl, and help Daddy out," he whispered, leaning over her.

As if she understood him, she took in a quivering breath then smiled, her teeth gleaming white in the darkened bedroom. Then she sucked in another breath, turned over in her crib, pulled her blanket around her face and released a gentle sigh of contentment.

Denny smiled as he straightened. Finally. He waited a moment longer, just to make sure. From the kitchen he heard the muted clink of plates as Evangeline loaded up the dishwasher, followed by the sound of running water. Sounds of home, he thought, backing out of the room and gently closing the door behind him.

Before joining Evangeline, however, he was curious to see if she had cleaned the room he'd told her to leave alone.

He flicked on the light and shook his head. Sure enough, the empty boxes that had littered the room were gone. The pink carpet had been vacuumed; the marks on the faded princess wallpaper wiped away. The bed, with its pink headboard and crown, was stripped, the mattress bare.

He paused a moment, trying to imagine Evangeline as a young girl staying here. She'd said she was eight when they'd moved.

One moment she was living in a happy home with two parents and her own pretty bedroom.

The next, her mother dead, her father dropping her off in town to live with a single woman who probably wasn't comfortable with kids.

Poor girl. He knew what it was like to have to leave a place you loved. At least he still had family.

He gently closed the door then walked down the hall. Evangeline was wiping the counter when he got to the kitchen.

"Ella go down okay?" she asked.

"Out like a light."

"I'm so glad she's sleeping better. Those teeth were really bothering her."

He nodded then smiled again as she rinsed out the cloth and hung it over the divider between the sinks.

He propped his shoulder against the door frame. He watched her working a moment, letting the thoughts that had roamed around the edges of his mind get closer to the foreground. Did he dare think something was building between them? Did he dare bring her into his life?

She dried her hands then turned to him. "So, did you want coffee or anything like that?"

He shook his head then angled his chin toward the living room. "I got the movie ready to go."

She waited for him to lead the way.

He had turned off all but one light and angled the love seat so it faced the television, an unspoken invitation for Evangeline to join him there. Thankfully she got the message and as he sat, she sank onto the seat beside him.

He hit the remote, laid it down and then, as easy as anything, slipped his arm across her shoulders. She sat still a moment, as if debating with herself what to do, then, thankfully, leaned against him.

A sense of fulfillment he hadn't felt in years slipped over him as the music began and the introductory credits flashed on the screen.

He looked over at Evangeline, surprised to see her looking at him instead of at the television.

"Aren't you watching the movie?" he asked.

"Aren't you?" she countered.

He brushed a strand of hair away from her face, the light from the screen flashing over her features. "I like it when you wear your hair loose like this," he murmured.

She smiled. "I'll keep that in mind."

He dragged his attention back to the movie but couldn't look away.

Evangeline was far more interesting to him, at this moment, than Sandra Bullock's adventures.

"I want to kiss you again," he said.

"Are you asking me or telling me?"

He let his fingers linger on her face, stroking her cheek gently, feeling guilty at the roughness of his fingers on the delicate softness of her skin.

"Warning you? Giving you a chance to stop me?"

Evangeline reached up and clasped her hand around his wrist, then turned her face into the palm of his hand, pressing her own kiss to it.

Denny's heart thudded heavily and began racing.

"I know we agreed to take our time, but I think we both know what's happening here," she said quietly, holding his hand against her cheek.

"Why don't you tell me?" he prompted.

Evangeline gave him a coy smile. "Why don't you?"

"I have a better idea." He bent closer, catching her lips in a gentle kiss followed by another, then another.

Her gentle response erased his misgivings. Created a sense of rightness and belonging. He cupped her face, his fingers caressing her cheek. "You light up my life, you know."

She gave him a careful smile, as if she hardly dared believe what he said. "Is this really happening? You and me."

He released a gentle sigh. "I hope so. I know I like being with you."

"I like being with you, too." She laid her head in the crook of his neck, her hand catching his and clinging to it. "We're missing the movie," she said.

"Then we'd better pay attention. I don't want to waste my money, after all."

She chuckled and nestled against him, her eyes on the television.

But as the movie played, he couldn't concentrate on the story line. He could only think of Evangeline lying in his arms and wondered if he dared make plans beyond this evening.

When the final credits rolled, he picked up the remote and clicked the television off.

"Thanks for the movie," Evangeline said, pulling away from him. "That was fun."

She sounded like a junior high school girl thanking her date.

"It was okay," Denny returned with a grin. "I think next time we should do the Three Stooges, though. I might actually pay attention."

Even in the dim light he could see her blush. He found it utterly beguiling. A woman who blushed.

"I should go," she said, slowly getting to her feet. "That alarm clock rings early in the morning."

Denny stood, as well, shoving his hands into

the back pockets of his jeans as he walked her to the door.

"Will you be bringing Ella to the store tomorrow?" she asked.

Denny shook his head as he held the door of the porch open for her. "I won't be working tomorrow. My truck broke down when the new guy was driving it."

When Carlos had called him with more truck trouble, he couldn't help feeling frustrated. Every minute counted with contract work.

But, somehow, it didn't bother him as much as it would have another time.

"So you won't need me then?" she asked as they walked in the cool of the evening to her car.

The sun had slipped behind the mountains, but it wasn't fully dark yet. And in the gathering dusk he easily read her expression.

Was she disappointed?

Denny gave her a slow smile. "Not to babysit, but if you want to stop by tomorrow again, that would be great. Only if you're not busy or if you have no other plans."

"I'd love to come by."

"Great. That would be great."

He hesitated, wondering if he should kiss her again. Then thought, why not? She hadn't objected the last time.

So he bent his head, brushed his lips over hers and slowly pulled back.

"See you tomorrow," she said, then ducked into her car and drove away.

Denny watched the taillights of her car go down the driveway, then flash as she braked before turning off onto the road.

He looked up into the sky.

"Am I doing the right thing?" he said aloud, his question a prayer. "Am I moving too quickly?"

He waited, but no answer floated down from above. He trudged back to his house, but even though he hadn't received any direction, he couldn't shake the feeling that what was happening between him and Evangeline was right.

Evangeline parked her car in her usual spot behind the bookstore and turned the engine off. In the quiet that followed, the only sound she heard was the far-off plaintive sound of a train's horn echoing through the valley.

The melancholy sound was at odds with the excitement thrumming through her.

Denny had kissed her again. She had kissed him back.

She reached her hand up to her lips as if to check for evidence of Denny's kiss. Then she smiled.

It was real. As was her reaction to him. Her

heart felt like bursting and her mind spun with thoughts of him.

She got out of the car, suddenly restless, needing to talk to someone. She looked up at the apartment above the flower shop beside hers.

A light was still on. Mia was still awake.

She hesitated, knowing how much Mia valued her quiet once she got all her kids into bed.

And yet…

Evangeline turned and climbed the wooden stairs at the back of the building leading to the outside entrance to Mia's apartment. She knocked on the door, lightly, in case Mia had left the light on and was in bed herself.

The door opened almost right away.

"Hey," Mia said, stepping back as she opened the door further. "Come on in."

"Are you sure?"

"Kids are down for the count. Renee took the boys swimming after supper and the twins didn't nap this afternoon, so everyone's tired."

Including you, thought Evangeline, concerned about the shadows under her friend's eyes.

"You're not just being polite?" Evangeline hesitated, not wanting to intrude.

"Please. I'm getting tired of my own company." Mia waved her in and then strode to the sink and filled the kettle with water. "Tea or hot chocolate?" she asked as she pulled a couple of mugs from her cupboard.

"Tea sounds good," Evangeline said, sitting at the table.

"So, where were you so late?" Mia asked, shooting Evangeline a mischievous look over her shoulder as she dropped the tea bags into the mugs.

"At the ranch."

"Was Ella fussy?"

"No. We…that is, me and Denny…we watched a movie."

"Sounds like fun," Mia said, taking out some cookies and setting them on a plate. "Which movie?"

Evangeline bit her lip, suddenly unable to remember.

"Right." Mia picked up an overflowing laundry basket from the table and set it aside.

"Do you want help with that?" Evangeline asked, gathering up the storybooks scattered on the table, as well.

"No. It will keep." Mia grinned, set the cookies on the table and leaned against the counter, waiting for the kettle. "So. You and Denny. Did he kiss you? Did you like it?"

"Mia," Evangeline scolded, feeling her cheeks warm again.

"I think you're the only person I know who

still blushes," Mia teased as she turned off the kettle and poured the boiling water into their mugs. "So delightfully old-fashioned."

Evangeline's only response was a quick shrug as Mia brought the mugs to the table.

"So, what brings you to my humble home?" Mia asked, dropping into her chair with a sigh. "You want to indulge in some of our usual girlie talk? Dissect the nuances of your conversations with him? What you said and what he said and what it may or may not have meant? How he smiled and what it made you feel like?"

Evangeline laughed at her friend's recitation of the things she'd often discussed with Mia when they were growing up.

Mia's eyes flashed with curiosity. "Is he a good kisser? Does he close his eyes? Put his hand on your shoulder or your cheek?"

"You sound like an investigative reporter."

"I was hoping I sounded like a police detective," Mia said. "Just finished reading our book club book and I'm still deep in the heroine's point of view."

"Any good?"

"I suppose you've been too busy with Mr. Norquest and his little baby girl to read it."

"I have." Evangeline sighed lightly. "And I don't know if I'm doing the right thing."

"So what's wrong with it?"

Evangeline stirred some honey into her tea, staring down at the amber liquid in her cup, trying to put words to the thoughts crowding her brain. "I don't think anything is. And that's the problem."

Mia held up her hand. "Whoa. Stop there. You lost me."

Evangeline took a sip of her tea and looked through the rising steam at her friend. She cradled her cup and shrugged. "I really like him. I'm fairly sure he likes me."

"He kissed you. I think you're beyond fairly sure."

"That's the trouble. I'm scared to think past that."

Mia chewed her lower lip. "Is this about Tyler?"

"And my previous boyfriend, Dave, and my father." Evangeline ran her finger along the edge of her mug, her concerns taking form. "It's like I keep latching my hopes on to the wrong person. And I'm afraid I'm doing the same thing with Denny."

"So you don't trust your judgment anymore."

Evangeline released a harsh laugh. "Not at all."

"Let's analyze this. Your other boyfriend, whatzis name, was a good-looking, suave kind of guy who had that tall, blond, Greek-god thing going for him. Tyler? Ditto." Mia ticked off her previous boyfriends' attributes on her fingers.

"They were your typical hero type. Successful in their field. Had money. Always dressed well. Neat and tidy life. But, basically, louses. Now there's Denny. Tall, yes, but dark. A bit scruffy. Drives a gravel truck. Had a kid dumped on his doorstep. A kid he never even knew about. Not the kind of hero you usually are drawn to."

"You make me sound superficial," Evangeline protested.

Mia shook her head. "Not superficial at all. Maybe just looking for love in the wrong place."

"And you think Denny is the right place? In many ways he reminds me of my father. Who, if you want to get analytical and psychological, was the first man who let me down."

Mia was quiet a moment. "Maybe in some ways he's like your dad. He drives a truck. He's a single dad. But I think there's a big difference. I hear you talk about him, how he is with Ella. Some of the sacrifices he's made for her." She released a short laugh, holding a bitter edge. "I think he's the real deal."

Evangeline pressed her lips together, then looked up at her friend. "But his life seems so… messy. I'm not holding it against him, but his divorce bothers me. I'm not narrow-minded about it, but it is part of his past."

"Ask him about it if you think it's a barrier."

"It's more of a concern. But you're right. I need to talk to him."

Mia's expression grew serious. "Everyone's life is messy. Neat and tidy only comes at the end of the story. You're in the middle of your own story and you can't see the end. Which is a good thing. I never pictured myself a single mother with four kids living above a flower shop, working my fingers to the bone, and no sign of a tidy ending. We keep going and hope and pray we make more good decisions than bad ones."

"I've made enough bad decisions in my life," Evangeline said.

"Haven't we all." Mia reached over and squeezed her friend's arm. "I know you gave Renee some good advice when she was struggling with what to do about Zach. You told her she deserved some happiness. Maybe you do, too. But maybe you need to adjust your idea of what that happiness should look like." She squeezed her arm again. "You like Denny. I know you do. I see your face light up when you talk about him like I never saw when you were dating Tyler. I think you went out with Tyler and Dave because they seemed an obvious fit. The hero you'd been looking for. The complete opposite of your father. Stable. Solid. Predictable. But when I hear you talk about Denny, I see a joy and spark I've never seen in you before."

Evangeline sat straighter, as if a burden of confusion had slipped off her shoulders.

"Can we do something we don't often do?" Mia asked, holding her friend's hand. "Can we pray together? I know your faith has been shaky of late, but I know I depend so heavily on God, maybe you need to, as well."

Evangeline gave her friend a thankful smile. "You're right. I do need to do that."

"Then let's pray," Mia said, reaching across the table and taking Evangeline's other hand in hers. Then she bowed her head.

"Dear Lord," she prayed. "Evangeline is so confused right now. Help her to know that You understand her seeking for order in the mess of our lives. Help her to cling to You, our rock and refuge in the turbulent times of our lives. The only wise God and Father. Help us all to trust in You, our God who holds us all in the palm of Your hands. Who will be beside and behind and before us in the decisions of our lives."

Evangeline let the prayer settle on her soul. God was her solid foundation. The Father she could trust in. Then she looked up at her friend and smiled. "Thanks, Mia. I knew I could count on your wisdom."

"Not so much wisdom," she said, shooting a glance around the cramped apartment. "Or else I wouldn't have ended up here." Her smile negated her morose tone. "Life is messy. But we have to muddle on as best we can and trust that if we make our decisions prayerfully, then God will guide us through them."

"Thanks, my friend." Evangeline glanced at the clock. "And I better go. You'll be up early tomorrow, I imagine. Kids have a way of keeping their own time."

"And you should know," Mia said. "But I'll keep praying for you. And give the guy a chance. I think he's gold."

Evangeline gave her friend a quick hug. "Thanks, Mia. You're a blessing."

She left the apartment feeling more confident, more certain she was moving in the right direction with Denny.

Chapter Eleven

"No, honey, don't eat that." Evangeline carefully pulled Ella's hand away from her mouth, chuckling at the dirt rimming her button mouth. Ella protested, clutching the stem of a weed that she waved around.

"Aren't kids supposed to eat a certain amount of fiber?" Denny grunted, pushing the shovel into the ground with his boot.

"Not before it's turned into carrots or vegetables," Evangeline said with a laugh as she extricated the weed from Ella's hand. Ella pouted but clambered to her feet and toddled off the blanket Evangeline had laid out for her to sit on. She was headed toward Denny, who was turning over the clump of dirt he had just dug up.

Evangeline wiped her hands on her pants, giving up on keeping her lemon-yellow capris clean. Ditto the white silk tank top with its beaded neckline.

When she found out what Denny had planned for the day she had removed her leather sandals and tied her hair back with the yellow-and-green scarf she had draped around her neck this morning and pitched in.

The pants were now liberally streaked with dirt as was the tank top. Sweat dripped down her temples and into her hair, but she didn't care.

Denny was working up her mother's flower beds. They were such a tangle of weeds and perennials, it was difficult to say where one ended and the other began. But Denny was slowly bringing order to the chaos.

"So that's this one," Denny said with a grunt as he tossed the last of the weeds onto the growing pile beside the flower bed. He straightened, placing his hand in the small of his back and flashing Evangeline a smile that created a flutter of joy.

"Now that you've taken the rock edging away, what are you putting in its place?" Evangeline caught Ella's hand before she stuck another handful of dirt in her mouth.

"I don't know, what do you think?"

Evangeline gave him a grateful smile. He wanted her input. As if she was a partner in the project.

It is your father's ranch, she reminded herself.

But at the same time, this was the first time

she'd been asked her opinion on anything to do with the house or the ranch.

"Brick would be nice," she said. "You can get some nice large bricks at the Hartley Creek nursery on the edge of town. The new owner is a bit of a grump, but he knows his stuff."

"We could go have a look later this afternoon, if that's okay with you?" Denny arched a questioning brow and Evangeline nodded, anticipation singing through her.

"Maybe we could get some new perennials?" Evangeline asked.

"If he still has them. It is getting late in the season to put them in. Fall might be a better time."

"How do you know so much about plants?"

Denny pulled out a hankie and wiped the sweat dripping down his face. "I helped my mother in the garden whenever I had time. She loved flowers, too. Working in the garden gave us time to talk. Share stuff." He shoved the hankie into his pocket, his face taking on a melancholy look as he glanced at Ella, who was pulling at Evangeline's hand, babbling away in her toddler jargon. "She was a good mother. She would have loved Ella."

Evangeline caught the note of longing in his voice, feeling a moment of kinship. Neither of them had a mother.

"I'm sure she would have," Evangeline murmured, swinging Ella up into her arms. "She's a sweetheart."

"Don't carry that little grublet," Denny warned, reaching out to take her away. "She's getting your fancy shirt dirty."

"Too late for that," Evangeline said, looking down at the smudges on her top. She gave him a quick grin. "So, is it time to take a lunch break?"

Denny glanced up at the sky, as if getting a reading from the sun. "I'm guessing it's about twelve-thirty."

"Your clock is slow," Evangeline teased, hefting Ella onto her hip as she glanced at the gold bracelet watch circling her wrist. "It's twelve thirty-six."

Denny laughed then reached over and gently wiped something off her cheek. "You had some dirt there," he said, but his fingers lingered, then flitted down her face, his hand coming to rest on her shoulder.

Evangeline leaned in, gave him a quick kiss, then grinning at his surprise, she turned and led the way into the house, unable to keep the smile off her face.

In a matter of minutes Ella was washed up and sitting in her high chair, gobbling up the pieces of bread Evangeline had buttered and cut up for her.

She set a plate of sandwiches out and a pitcher of lemonade with a set of mismatched glasses.

"Looks good," Denny said appreciatively as she sat. As natural as can be, he reached out for her hand and Ella's and bent his head to pray.

Evangeline followed suit, her heart warming.

"Thank You, Lord, for our food, for the hands that prepared it," Denny prayed. "For this beautiful day and Your creation that You bless us with. Amen."

"Amen," Evangeline breathed, pulling in a deep breath of satisfaction. She looked at Denny, his hair still damp from the water he'd splashed over his head, his face shining from washing up, his eyes holding a glimmer of satisfaction.

Stubble shaded his jaw and his hair could use a cut. His shirt was ragged at the collar and the cuffs were worn. And none of that mattered.

He really was a handsome man, Evangeline thought.

Could this be happening? Could she possibly be ready to give her heart to him? He was so different from what she had long considered her ideal.

He looked up and gave her a warm smile that created a fan of crinkles around deep brown eyes framed by shaggy hair.

And she realized how her "ideal" had changed.

"So, I think we can finish up the other side after lunch," Denny said, picking up a piece of bread Ella had tossed on the floor. "After that's done, I thought we could head into town to get what we need to edge the beds. If that's okay with you?"

"More than okay. Ella won't need a nap for a while, so that should work."

"When we get back I'd like to rototill the garden."

"I don't think the tiller works." Evangeline gave Ella a piece of fruit. "I don't think anyone's used it since…since my father and I left."

"I had it running a couple of nights ago," Denny said, wiping some crumbs off his mouth. "Needed a new spark plug, new filters and a good grease job, but that was it."

She shook her head. "You constantly amaze me," she said.

"I like the sound of that. I haven't amazed too many people in my life of late."

The edge in his voice made her wonder if he was talking about his ex-wife. She took another bite of her sandwich, thinking about what she and Mia had talked about the other night. She had been waiting for the right time. Maybe it was now.

"I take it you mean Lila?" she asked hesitantly.

"Her least of all."

The harsh tone in his voice almost made her change her mind, but if she and Denny were moving in the direction she thought, she needed to know about his past relationship.

"Was your marriage very difficult?"

Denny shot her a frown. "Why do you want to know?"

"I'm curious. Just trying to find out more about you."

Denny gave Ella a piece of cut-up banana Evangeline had put in a bowl for her. Then he sighed. "Lila is a part of my past I prefer not to talk about."

"But she's Ella's mother." Evangeline kept her voice quiet. Nonthreatening. Denny's jaw grew tight and for a moment she regretted bringing up the subject.

"How did you meet her?" she prompted.

Denny blew out a sigh and then leaned back in his chair, his arms crossed, his fingers beating out an irregular rhythm on his arm. "We met in a bar. I was in a bad place in my life and not living the way I should." He stopped there, as if hoping Evangeline would give him an out, but she simply waited. Thankfully Ella was engrossed in trying to smear bananas into her mouth rather than eat them and wasn't paying attention to either of them.

"My parents had been dead a few years," Denny continued, his eyes taking on a far-off look, as if delving into the past he didn't want to discuss. "I was working myself to the bone trying to keep the ranch going, my sisters and Nate out of trouble and my uncle happy. Wasn't doing great at any of it, but I knew I couldn't quit. I would take off in the evenings and weekends to get away from the demands. That's when I met Lila. She was pretty. She was interested in me. She laughed at my stupid jokes and made me feel important. Special." He released a harsh laugh. "As if that isn't the biggest cliché ever." He stopped there, but Evangeline only gave Ella another piece of banana.

"Anyhow, we…we got together." This was followed by another sigh and Evangeline guessed what he meant by his vague phrasing. "Like I said, not a good time in my life. I was not exactly on speaking terms with God."

"Because of losing your parents," she said quietly.

He nodded. "About three months after we started dating, she told me she was pregnant. So I stepped up to my responsibilities. I married her and moved her out to the ranch. Found out she wasn't pregnant. She'd only wanted to get married. Thought I was some rich rancher and could provide all the things she wanted. Didn't take her long to figure out that wasn't true. She wanted out, but I thought we should keep trying. We tried for five years."

He stopped there, his fingers quiet as his eyes took on a dull, sad look. "But she insisted she wanted a divorce. I tried to talk her out of it. I had returned to my faith and had made promises I had to keep. Toward the end we spent a couple of weeks…together. I'm sure that's when she got pregnant with Ella. Then she left and next thing I knew I was being served with divorce papers. Trouble was, because we'd been married five years she was entitled to a fair amount of support. We agreed to a lump sum but I had to sell the ranch to satisfy the terms of the divorce."

Evangeline felt dread shiver through her. "I'm so sorry, Denny. I didn't know."

"How could you?" He released another humorless laugh and put his hand on Ella's little shoulder. Then he bent over and kissed her golden curls. "But I got Ella out of the deal. So maybe, in the end, God had it all worked out."

He gave her a quick look, then away. "So, now that you know the details of my sordid and chaotic past—"

She was about to reassure him that she didn't see it as sordid or chaotic at all. In fact she found his devotion to the promises he made touching. Heroic.

But a loud knocking on the door broke into the moment. The door flew open and she didn't have an opportunity to formulate her thoughts as the sound of laughter and voices filled the porch.

"Honey, we're home!" one of the voices shouted from the porch.

Female and young, Evangeline thought.

Ella twisted in her high chair to see who was disturbing her lunch.

"Olivia? Trista?" Denny called out, getting up from his seat as the door from the porch flew open and two girls burst into the room.

"Hey, big brother," the shorter girl greeted, her grin blindingly white against her tanned skin as she dropped her backpack on the floor. She wore khaki shorts, a loose gray shirt over a camo tank top and leather sandals.

She ran over to him, her long brown hair flying behind her as she threw her arms around him. "Missed you." She gave him a tight hug and pulled back, brushing his hair back from his face. "And you need a haircut, don't you think, Trista?"

The second girl, Trista, was taller, with short blond hair that stuck up in spikes of gelled hair. She was dressed identically except for a T-shirt with a picture of a yellow baby chick on a sandy beach, the words proclaiming that she was one hot chick.

"Olivia, stop hogging Denny," Trista said, elbowing her sister aside and planting a noisy kiss on Denny's cheek, framing his face with her hands. "There. We're back."

"I see that. So when—"

"So this is the little munchkin," Olivia interrupted, bending over Ella. Then, as she lifted the little girl out of the high chair, she shot Evangeline a puzzled glance. "And you are?"

Evangeline suppressed her annoyance at Denny's sister's question. As if she was a stranger here when, in fact, it was her father's house they had just invaded.

But her manners kicked in and she stood, reaching out a hand in greeting. "I'm Evangeline Arsenau."

"Olivia," the young girl said, holding out one hand, bouncing Ella in her other arm as she started to fuss. "Hey, baby. I'm your auntie," Olivia said, looking down at the little girl with a huge grin. "And you are perfectly adorable. Don't you think she looks exactly like Adrianna when she was a baby?" Olivia turned Ella to Trista as if showing off some prize.

"Oh, man. Yeah." Trista wrinkled her nose at Ella. "Hey, baby girl. Say hi to your auntie Trista."

Evangeline looked from the girls who had taken over the house to Denny, who stood to one side, his hands on his hips, one corner of his mouth tucked between his teeth. He took in a long breath, his shoulders lifting then lowering as he blew out a sigh. "Sorry about this," he murmured to Evangeline. "I had given up on Olivia."

"Oh, never give up on me, big brother," Olivia protested, looking up from tickling Ella under the chin. "I may be slow but I'm sure."

Denny didn't say anything to that. Instead he shoved one hand through his hair and looked from Olivia to Trista. "Are you girls hungry? Do you need some lunch?"

"That would be awesome," Olivia said, plopping down at the table, still holding Ella, who didn't seem to mind the sudden invasion in her life.

"Sandwich okay?" Denny asked as he walked over to the kitchen counter.

Trista nodded then sat beside her sister as Denny tugged the twist tie off the loaf of bread.

"I can take care of that," Evangeline said, taking the bag from him, surprised his sisters didn't offer to help.

"I don't mind," he said. "I'm used to it."

She glanced back at the girls then gently took the jar of mayonnaise out of his hand, nudging him with her elbow. "Go visit with your sisters. I'll make some sandwiches."

He hesitated and she was about to nudge him again when he finally stepped back.

"Trista doesn't like mayo on her sandwich and

Olivia doesn't like mustard," he murmured as Evangeline twisted the top off the jar.

"Duly noted," she said, giving him a quick grin.

His lopsided smile created a gentle warmth in her heart. "Thanks, Evangeline. I'm sorry about the deluge. If I had known they were both coming…" He let the sentence drift off as if he wasn't entirely sure what he would have done in that case.

Evangeline shot a quick look over her shoulder at the two girls cooing over Ella, laughing as they bounced her up and down. "They seem to be fun-loving girls."

"That they are. Again, I'm sorry."

"Don't worry about it. It's fine. Go visit."

His hand briefly lingered on her shoulder then he did as she told him, walked back to the table and dropped down in a chair by the girls.

As Evangeline worked, her attention was drawn by the animated conversation going on behind her. She smiled as she heard them laugh as Olivia and Trista shared stories with their brother about their adventures.

They talked about Adrianna, their other sister, about friends from back home that Olivia and Trista had run into. With each conversation and shared joke and laugh she felt increasingly edged out.

When Evangeline set the plate of sandwiches on the table and laid the napkins beside them she got a murmured thank-you from the girls and another apologetic look from Denny as the girls returned to their storytelling.

She put the bread away, cleaned up the ham and cheese and condiments, then wiped the counter, feeling rather out of place as she finished, not sure what she was supposed to do.

"Hey, Evangeline, if you want to get back to your own work in town, I'm here now," Olivia put in as Evangeline rinsed the cloth out and hung it over the sink divider to dry.

"We were heading to the garden center," Denny put in as Evangeline returned to the table. "To get some plants to put in the flower bed in the front of the house."

Olivia waved his comment off. "She doesn't look like she's dressed for that kind of work," she said, looking at Evangeline's outfit. "I'm sure you roped her into helping like you always did with us."

Olivia turned to Evangeline with a bright smile. "I know I was supposed to come sooner but Trista and I got a week of overtime work and now we're done for the year. So you don't need to work here anymore."

Though Evangeline was sure Denny had told Olivia this before things had changed between them, she couldn't stop the flick of hurt Olivia's words gave her.

However, to act differently would be to arouse suspicion.

And Evangeline wasn't ready to let Denny's sisters wonder what was happening between her and Denny. She wanted to guard her changing feelings. To hold them close. She felt as if bringing them out for other's scrutiny would diminish them.

"Then I'll head back to town," she said, avoiding Denny's disappointed look.

"You don't have to leave," he protested.

"I've got a bunch to do, so this works out fine," she said. She wasn't lying about that. She had been neglecting some of the more mundane chores in the store of late because she had been spending so much time with Denny and Ella.

"Will I see you on Sunday?" he asked.

His question sent expectation coursing through her.

Her eyes met his. She nodded. "I'll be in church" was all she would say.

She turned her attention back to his sisters. "It was lovely meeting you. I hope you have a nice visit with your brother." She flashed them a quick smile, then hurried out the door before they could ask more questions.

But as she drove away she felt as if the situation had shifted and she knew Denny's priorities would change. That was the way it should be, but for a moment she wished his sisters had waited longer before coming.

Denny shoved the spade into the flower bed then held the dirt aside as his sister set the lily root into the ground. After Evangeline had left, Trista had stayed behind to watch Ella while he and Olivia went to the nursery. Though he had been waiting for his sister to come to help, he was unhappy with Olivia's timing.

Things were shifting, changing between him and Evangeline, and he wanted to take the time to see where it would go. He didn't want to rush things.

His sisters' presence would definitely put a damper on that particular plan.

"And that's the last of them," Olivia said, resting back on her heels, her hands on her hips as she surveyed the newly planted flower beds. Then she glanced up at Denny as she got to her feet. "This place is looking good already. You look like you're putting down some of your own roots for a change."

"Just trying to take care of the place," Denny said as he tamped the dirt around the base of the plant.

"Looks like you're doing more than that," Olivia teased, bending to pick up a shovel.

She straightened, pushing her hair back from her face, leaving a streak of dirt on her cheek. "So. Tell me about this Evangeline chick. She anything special to you?"

Denny kept tamping, avoiding his sister's probing gaze. "Can you take the spades and rakes to that shed beside the barn?" he asked. "I've got to head out and check the fences on the upper pasture before I turn the cows loose there."

"She's nothing like the girls you are usually attracted to." Olivia's voice held a serious note, completely at odds with her usual, ever-present humor.

"Well, she's nothing like Lila."

"I'm talking about some of the girls you dated in high school," Olivia said, ignoring his comment about his previous wife. "The outdoorsy, fun-loving, casual country girls you hung around with."

"How is she different?" Denny brushed the dirt off his pants, fully aware of what Olivia was hinting at but waiting for her perspective on the situation.

"I don't know. She seems kind of fancy. Likes to dress nice. And that snazzy car of hers…"

"She got it from her father," Denny said defensively.

"Daddy's little girl," Olivia said with a smirk. "That's a tough one."

Denny wanted to defend Evangeline but at the same time Olivia's words snaked into his thoughts and dug up his own insecurities about Evangeline. "She's hardly Daddy's girl," he said, taking the shovels and rakes from Olivia. "He's never around."

"But his money seems to be."

Denny leaned on the rake handle, holding Olivia's eyes. "Why don't you say what you want to say?"

Olivia lifted her shoulder in a slow shrug. "I saw how you two looked at each other. I'm guessing there's something going on between you two. But I love you, Denny. And you made a bad choice before. Make sure you don't make another one."

"You think Evangeline would be a bad choice?" His voice took on an edge he instantly regretted. Olivia was just being a sister.

Olivia held up her hand. "No. She seems awesome. But I look at her clothes and her car and those pearls around her neck and I'm thinking she's out of your league."

"She's not rich."

"No. I'm not saying that. But I think she's used to things a certain way. I can't see her living here and enjoying it."

Even as Denny's own defense of Evangeline rose to his lips, his mind skipped back to comments Andy had made about keeping his little princess happy. He thought of the bedroom in the house, the clothes Evangeline favored.

The car she drove.

In spite of her reaction to her father, she seemed to have no qualms about taking the gifts he gave her.

"At least she's been here for me," Denny continued in her defense. "She's done stuff for me and Ella that no one else could or would." Implying that his sisters were lacking in the "helping" department.

Olivia folded her arms, her eyes steady on him. Then she released a slow breath. "I'm just saying be careful. Now Ella is your first responsibility. You can't afford to be with the wrong person."

Denny looked at his little sister, trying to figure out how to respond. Coming from Olivia, who never put anyone but herself first, her comment was ironic.

But in spite of that he knew she was speaking the truth. Then a cry from the house reinforced what she was saying. "I'll go see what's wrong," Olivia said. "You go fix your fences."

As Denny walked back to the shed beside the barn, he experienced a beat of resentment. Olivia was right but he felt as if he was back to putting everyone else first as he had most of his life.

No sooner did the thought form than guilt struck at him.

"Please forgive me, Lord," he prayed. "I love Ella. I do. It's just she got dropped into my life right when I wanted to be on my own. I'm still learning how to take care of her."

That Evangeline had come into his life at the same time was either a blessed coincidence or bad timing.

He hooked the rakes and spades on the nails he had pounded into the wall and strode to the tack shed. He needed to get on his horse and head out. Clear his head from the second thoughts and worries tangling his mind the past few weeks.

But as he saddled his horse, and later as he rode through the valley along the fence line, his thoughts shifted back to how Evangeline had looked that afternoon she'd brought him here to the ranch. The yearning on her face as she'd looked over the property, the longing in her voice.

She would like it here. She did like it here. She grew up here.

And he cared for Evangeline. He wanted to spend time with her. Then an idea came to him.

His sisters were here now and he needed to take advantage of that.

He was going to take Evangeline on a date. Just the two of them. No Ella. No other obligations.

He smiled at the thought, then reached down

to stroke his horse's neck. "I think it will be all right, Chester," he said, easing out a gentle sigh. "I think it will be just fine."

Chapter Twelve

"Morning, Olivia," Denny said as he walked into the kitchen Sunday morning, buttoning up the cuff of his shirt.

His little sister sat by the table, engrossed in one of the outdoors magazines she favored. He had always figured Olivia could live outside. She hiked, camped, rafted, canoed, skied and snowshoed whenever she could. Even the jobs she took kept her outdoors.

Olivia looked up from the article she was reading. "Hey, big brother. Are you all dressed up for church?" Olivia asked.

As dressed up as he could get, Denny thought, looking down at his clean blue jeans and newest cotton shirt. He didn't own a tie or suit and while that never bothered him before, today he was meeting Evangeline, who always looked like an ad for women's perfume. However, this was the best he could do.

"I am, but I need some help. Ella isn't feeling well, so I was wondering if you or Trista could stay at home this morning and watch her."

Olivia pursed her lips as if considering. "Trista and I wanted to check out a hike this magazine wrote about." She pointed to a picture of the Three Sisters, a mountain overlooking Hartley Creek. "Looks like it could be challenging and interesting."

Denny tried not to let his momentary annoyance show. "I thought you came to help me out."

"Well, yeah. I did. But…this is such an amazing place and there's so much to do. Trista and I have been working ourselves ragged the past few months. We were hoping to have a break."

In spite of his aggravation with Olivia, he felt his resolve waver. He knew she'd been busy. She'd lost weight since he'd seen her last and the weariness in her usually sparkling eyes disturbed him.

He wanted to talk to her, but he couldn't yet.

"I know. But so was I," Denny said, feeling the need to stand firm. "And you came here to help me out."

Olivia gnawed at her fingernail, another sure sign that things were not well in his little sister's world. "I suppose. And I said I would help but…" Her voice wavered then trailed off.

Don't give in, Denny thought. *You need to go to church and Ella isn't feeling well.*

So he said nothing while he waited for his sister to, for once, think about someone else besides herself.

"I guess I could stay this morning," Olivia said, glancing longingly at the magazine again. "But you'll be back after church, won't you?"

Denny had hoped he could take Evangeline out for lunch. To spend some time with her away from Ella and away from obligations.

Just an ordinary date. Something he hadn't had for years.

"I might be longer than that. I think you and Trista can help me out here."

Olivia's slow shrug wasn't encouraging but he persisted. "I haven't asked much from you girls," he said, keeping his voice quiet and reasonable. "I think I can ask this."

"Ask what?" Trista asked as she entered the room. Her hair stuck out in all directions, looking even more ragged than it had when they'd first showed up.

"Denny wants us to babysit this morning," Olivia said.

"I thought we were going on that Three Sister's hike," Trista said, then yawned and stretched out her arms. She looped one around Denny and planted a kiss on his cheek. "Hey, big brother, you're looking all shaved and polished. Is this for that Evangeline chick?"

"That's why he wants us to babysit. He's going to church," Olivia said. "He won't be back until lunchtime."

"Maybe later," Denny warned.

"But that hike will take most of the day," Trista said.

"So do it another day. Or, better yet, one of you could come to church with me."

Trista paused a moment, then shrugged the suggestion off. Her casual attitude toward church bothered him. He and his uncle had raised both girls better than that. "Not today" was all she said.

"We can't go hiking tomorrow 'cause you're working, and I thought you wanted us to take care of Ella during the week," Olivia put in.

Denny inhaled a long breath, his patience running out. "Here's the deal. You girls are staying here and I'd like something in return for that. This morning I want to go to church. After church I'm taking Evangeline out for lunch. Maybe next Saturday I'll be able to take a day off so you girls can do this hike. In the meantime, you'll have to figure out something else to do this afternoon that won't take as long."

His eyes moved from one to the other, as if to reinforce what he was saying.

Trista shrugged and sat on a chair, pulling one leg up to her chest and looping her arm around it. "Okay. Whatever."

Olivia fingered the corner of her magazine then sighed. "Sure. I guess."

"Thanks, girls," he said, trying to keep the thin note of sarcasm out of his voice at their less than enthusiastic agreement. "Ella is sleeping right now. She had a bad night, so let her sleep. She can have some hot cereal for breakfast, and feed her some banana. Diapers and wipes are in her bedroom. I've set out her clothes already."

"Wow. Mr. Mom," Trista said with awe.

"I have my moments."

Trista's mouth curved in a lazy smile. "I remember you getting our clothes ready for school," she said. "Those were good times. Fun times."

Though he was thankful his sister had good memories of those years, Denny had a different take on those supposed "good times." The responsibility of three sisters, a foster brother and a ranch had been a huge weight. There hadn't been much fun for him.

He brushed the negative thoughts aside. That was from another time and another place in his life. Things, right now, were looking better.

"I'll see you girls later. I'll send you a text when I'm coming home."

Olivia shrugged, obviously not happy with this, but she turned her attention back to the magazine. Trista gave him a languid wave. "Have fun," she said. "Say a prayer for me."

"I always do," he said.

"I know," Trista said with a melancholy smile. "You're a good brother."

He returned her smile, his momentary pique with his sisters easing away.

But he grabbed his corduroy jacket, tossed it over his shoulder, then left before either of his dear sisters could change her mind.

As the final notes of the song faded away Evangeline released a sigh of perfect peace. The church service had nourished, encouraged and challenged her.

Having Denny standing beside her had added to the sense of wonder she had felt the past few days.

She chanced another look at him and felt a shiver of awareness as she caught his warm look, which was as real as a touch.

"Do you have plans for lunch?" he asked her as they waited to exit the row.

"I have inventory to do and books to return, but there's no rush on either job." She gave him a careful smile, not sure she wanted to assume he was asking her to lunch but at the same time giving herself some space to accept.

"Great. I was thinking we could go to the restaurant by the ski lodge. They have a great Sunday brunch on today. I could drive you or we could meet there."

Evangeline's smile blossomed. "Let's meet there."

He grinned, then, as she walked past him, his hand lingering a moment on her shoulder, sending a shiver trickling down her neck and back.

"Hey, friend," Renee called. As she caught up to Evangeline her gaze slid from her to Denny. "Carter and Emma are having a barbecue. All the Beck grandkids will be there. Hailey, Dan and Natasha. Carter, Emma and Adam. Larissa and Garret and Naomi and Jess. It'll be a great party. Zach and I are invited and Emma asked me to invite you, as well. You, too, Denny. If you're interested?"

A few months ago the idea of being with so many happy couples would have depressed Evangeline.

But now the idea held an appeal. Now she had someone who would be at her side.

She looked over at Denny, who simply shrugged, giving her the option.

Evangeline turned back to Renee. "It sounds like fun but Denny and I have other plans."

Renee gave her a knowing grin. "Maybe we can catch you two another time."

You two.

Those simple words created a subtle undertow of pleasure.

"That would be nice," Evangeline said, pleased to think there might be another time for her and Denny. "And what did you and Larissa decide about the table settings at your meeting?"

They walked out of church together, chatting. Denny walked silently behind them, seemingly content to listen to Renee and Evangeline talk wedding plans.

A few minutes and a few topics later, she and Renee parted ways.

"You're really a part of this community, aren't you?" Denny said as he pulled his keys out of the pocket of his jeans.

"I've lived here all my life," Evangeline said, giving him a gentle smile, appreciating the way his eyes crinkled at the corners, the shine of his freshly shaved cheeks and chin. "It's my community."

"Community is a real blessing." His voice took on a poignant tone.

"So is family," Evangeline put in, thinking of his sisters and how easily they'd made themselves at home. How quickly they were comfortable because Denny was there.

"I'd argue with you on that one," Denny said. He spun his keys around his finger and, to her surprise and utter pleasure, he bent over and brushed a quick kiss over her lips. It was the merest whisper of a kiss but doing it in such a public place kindled a gentle warmth in her soul.

Fifteen minutes later Evangeline pulled up beside Denny's truck at the ski lodge, anticipation singing through her. This was the first time they were spending time together without Ella.

They were seated quickly in a quiet alcove, given the menus and thankfully left alone.

"Do you want to do the buffet brunch?" Denny asked, glancing at the menus on the table.

Evangeline didn't want to do anything but stay with Denny, so she shook her head. "If it's okay with you, I'll order."

"Sounds more than okay," Denny said, taking a menu and giving her one, as well.

Their waitress returned a few minutes later with their water and tea, then took their orders.

"So, how is Ella?" she asked when their waitress left.

"She wasn't feeling well. That's why I got Olivia to babysit. Though that was like pulling teeth."

Evangeline frowned in confusion.

"She and Trista supposedly had other plans."

He released a sigh as he took her hand in his. "Anyhow, I don't want to talk about them or Ella. I want you to know that I've never been as happy as I am when I'm with you," he said.

His words drifted into the empty and lonely parts of her heart. "I feel the same way," she replied.

Denny slid his fingers down her cheek, lingering by her lips. The intimacy of his actions brought a smile to her face.

"I know I'm not exactly the Prince Charming type," he said with a light laugh. "My life is a mess and every time I get my feet under me something else throws me off balance."

"You have had a lot to deal with," she agreed. "But you are a good man, Denny. The way you take care of Ella—the way you've learned to take care of her—is admirable. It makes you a hero in my eyes." She caught herself there, aware of the sudden intensity in her voice. But she felt she needed to assure him. "I'm not that shallow. I can see who you really are. I'm not waiting for some lord or duke to sweep me off my feet, though if you were one, I wouldn't object."

Denny's smile filled her heart. "Sorry. No duke, prince or lord here. Just a truck driver slash rancher."

"No 'just' about it," Evangeline said, laying a finger on his lips as if to stop him.

"So you don't mind that I ended up with a baby I didn't know about, family members who drop in and out of my life like rain? Sometimes welcome, sometimes not?"

Evangeline chuckled. "I think you need to see that family of yours as a blessing. Trust me, I would have loved to have someone else in my life. One is a pretty lonely number when you grow up that way."

"Five isn't lonely," he returned with a wry smile. "And now I have Ella, as well."

"Ella is a sweetheart."

"You like her, don't you?"

"More than like her," Evangeline assured him. "I will miss having her around the store all day. She's pretty special."

"I'm glad about that. I don't think she's going anywhere. And now that Olivia is around maybe you and I will have some time to figure out—" He stopped there. He looked down at their joined hands, his brows lowered as if concerned.

"To figure out what?" she gently prodded.

Denny waited a moment, as if sorting out what he was going to say. "To figure out our relationship."

"In terms of…?" Evangeline coaxed.

He released a gentle sigh. "I've made mistakes before and—" He bit his lip as if hesitant to speak his next words and she felt a barb hook into her heart.

"You don't want to make a mistake with me?" She tried to keep her voice light, as if speaking those words didn't cost her everything.

"I have to be careful," Denny said, but he still held her hands, which gave her hope. "But at the same time I'm sure you and I...that we can—"

"Evangeline. How nice to see you again."

That voice. The timing.

Evangeline gritted her teeth then forced a smile as she faced her old boyfriend.

Tyler wore his usual well-tailored suit; navy with a narrow white pinstripe. His white shirt set off his tanned skin and the indigo silk tie brought out the blue of his eyes. But the tan, she knew, came from a salon.

At one time that hadn't mattered, but as she looked from Tyler—perfectly groomed, perfectly put together—to Denny, who looked far more casual, she wondered what she'd seen in a man who, she knew, spent so much time on himself.

Tyler suddenly seemed fake.

Denny, real.

"Good afternoon, Tyler. Good to see you." It wasn't. His timing was atrocious and his presence unwelcome.

Tyler fingered the lapel of his suit jacket with a manicured hand, lifting one eyebrow in question.

Evangeline's manners returned. "Tyler, this is Denny Norquest. He rents my father's ranch. Denny, this is Tyler Wright. A…a friend."

Tyler gave her a slow smile. "Only friend? I thought we were more than that." Tyler turned to Denny. "Evangeline and I dated for many years."

It was growing harder to keep her smile intact. Tyler's smooth, deep voice suddenly struck her as obsequious and his comment to Denny possessive.

"Thankfully we've both moved on," Evangeline returned, looking pointedly at Denny.

"I see that." But the edge in Tyler's voice made her wonder what had happened to the girl he had dumped her for. But she wasn't asking, because she wasn't interested.

"Thanks for stopping by," she said to Tyler, her smile suddenly genuine and relieved.

What had she seen in this man? Compared to Denny he seemed fussy and shallow.

Denny, with his so-called messy life, was the genuine article. A diamond in the rough, maybe. But more precious than Tyler ever was.

"I saw you come into the restaurant," he said, "and wanted to say hello. Maybe I'll see you around?"

"Hartley Creek isn't that big" was all she would say, wishing he would leave. She knew her time with Denny, time snatched away from his many obligations, was precious. She didn't want to waste it on a man who no longer held her interest.

Tyler's smile grew tight, as if he knew she had brushed him off. Then with a nod in Denny's direction he said goodbye and walked away.

"So. Old boyfriend." Denny's comment held a note of asperity, which made Evangeline smile even more. "Your dad mentioned him once or twice."

"I'm sure he did," Evangeline said. "My dad liked Tyler."

Denny released a sound that sounded suspiciously like a snort.

Was he jealous?

"We dated for two years," she said.

"That's a long time to be with someone."

"That's three years less than you were married," she put in, reminding him she wasn't the only one with past relationships.

"Touché," Denny said.

"He's not important, if that's what you're wondering," she said.

"I was and I'm glad to hear that. Really glad."

"Why?" she asked, fishing for an answer she was fairly sure she already knew.

"Because I was hoping you could tell me that I'm more important."

Evangeline laughed, then leaned closer, caught

his neck and pressed a kiss to his lips. "There. Does that help?"

"It's a beginning," he said, his smile growing. Then he kissed her back.

As his lips touched hers she felt a completeness in her soul. Tyler had dealt her a blow that had resonated through her life.

And now?

Now she was with a man she admired. Whom she cared more deeply for than she had ever cared for any man.

The realization hit her like a blow. She pulled back and tightened her hand on his, feeling vulnerable and afraid.

Dear Lord, she prayed silently, *let me have chosen right.*

Because she felt, now more than at any other time in her life, she was putting her heart in the hands of someone who had the potential to hurt her more than anyone else ever had.

Chapter Thirteen

Denny watched Evangeline pull out onto the highway leading back to Hartley Creek, thankful for the warm afternoon sun after the cool dimness of the restaurant.

He had enjoyed his afternoon with Evangeline. Being with her felt right and good. She was the kind of person he had always dreamed of being with. The kind of woman he had hoped to marry first time around.

"Hey, Norquest."

Denny turned to see Tyler striding toward him across the parking lot, his smile showing perfectly straight teeth. "How was your lunch with Evangeline?" Tyler asked as he came near.

"It was good," Denny returned, fidgeting with his truck keys.

Tyler ran his hand over the lapels of a suit Denny figured had been tailored specifically for him. The guy looked like an ad for expensive men's cologne.

"You and Evangeline seemed kind of cozy," Tyler said. "Are you serious about her?"

"I don't see that's any of your business," Denny returned.

"She was a part of my life," Tyler said.

"Was. For two years. And then you dumped her. Big mistake."

"You're right. It was a mistake. I miss her. She's such a perfect person." Then he released a harsh laugh that held no humor. "You don't seem like Evangeline's type. She always told me she didn't like the rough and rugged sort. Reminded her too much of her father. Come to think of it, you do kind of remind me of Andy."

Denny didn't think the comment required a response, yet Tyler's words struck a chord. He knew he was more like Evangeline's father than Tyler was. Denny fell short in many ways of Evangeline's ideal.

"I had better be going," Denny said. "Got to get back to the ranch." He knew he was being curt with Evangeline's old boyfriend. The guy gave him the willies with his cologne and perfect skin and clothes. He reminded him too much of one of the lawyers Lila had hired.

"Have a good day," Tyler said with a forced smile. Without another word, Tyler turned and walked away, leaving Denny to wonder what the guy had really wanted.

He didn't have time to wonder too much. His cell phone was buzzing at him. He glanced at the number and felt his heart slow. Andy. Evangeline's father.

"Hey, Denny. How's it going? You working right now?" Andy asked him

"I'm out and about." He wasn't about to tell Andy that he had taken his daughter out to lunch. Somehow he didn't think Andy would approve. Andy had mentioned Tyler once in a while and Denny had the idea that Evangeline's father would have preferred it if she was still dating him.

"Got a few minutes?" Andy asked. "I need to run something by you."

"Go ahead," Denny said as he got into his truck, rolled down the window and propped his elbow on the edge. From here he could see the river that flowed through town, could hear it splashing over the rocks, moving relentlessly onward.

Andy was quiet a moment, which generated a slow beat of concern.

"It's about the ranch. We need to talk about the terms," Andy said.

The beat quickened, filling his chest.

"What about the terms?"

"Well, I did tell you I'd give you five-year lease. I need to change that."

Denny closed his eyes and pinched the bridge of his nose, concern morphing into dread. "How do you want to change it?" Denny guessed Andy didn't want to lengthen it.

"I was thinking you could buy me out in the next month."

The dread turned into ice curling through his veins. "Buy you out now?"

"This guy told me about a real-estate deal he wants to put together. I can double my money in less than a year. Which means I could sign over the store to Evangeline. I could come back to Hartley Creek and give her everything I've wanted."

Which is what Evangeline had been waiting for all these years. While Denny was happy for her, thrilled for her, in fact, he couldn't say he felt the same way about his own situation.

"I can't come up with that kind of money right now," Denny said. "The lease agreement gave me just enough room to save up a down payment."

"What about your trucks? What if you sold them?"

"I need the income from them to get my stake together." There was no way he was buying a ranch, diving deep into debt and scrabbling his way out of that black hole for the rest of his life. Especially not if his life was moving in the direction he had hoped.

Together with Evangeline.

He had no intention of subjecting her to that kind of subsistence living. He had scrambled enough when he and Lila were married and look where that had got him.

"You sure you couldn't shorten the lease to three years?" Denny countered. That would give him some breathing room. Not as much as he'd like, but enough.

"I need the money now, Denny. It's a great opportunity."

"And if I don't buy you out?"

"I have to sell the ranch one way or the other. Sorry."

He didn't sound sorry and Denny finally, truly, realized what Evangeline had had to deal with most of her life. Andy didn't have the guts to tell him this to his face. He had to do it over the phone.

"Give me a day or so to think about this," Denny said. "I need to make some plans."

"Sure. But I'm under the gun. I need to get some kind of assurance by the end of the week. I can borrow the money but only if I know I'll be able to pay it back when you get financing for the ranch."

"Even if I do get financing, it won't happen for

a while. I can't just waltz into the bank and get them to hand over that kind of money."

"I'm okay with that. I don't mind carrying the loan if I know money's coming. I trust you, Denny."

Which was more than Denny could say for Andy.

"Like I said, give me a couple of days. I need to figure a few things out."

"Say hi to my girl, will you?"

Denny clenched his teeth, his frustration and anger with Andy spilling over.

"Why don't you come up for a visit and say hi to her yourself?" he asked.

A moment of silence followed his outburst and Denny figured he had overstepped an invisible boundary.

"I know. I should."

"She misses you," Denny said, surprised at the chastened tone he heard in Andy's voice.

"I'll come up when I can sign the store over to her. When this deal is through."

"Does transferring ownership of the store to her depend on this deal?"

"I won't need the income from the store once I get this deal together."

That put another angle on the situation. Added another complication. Denny knew what that store meant to Evangeline.

"I'll talk to you by Wednesday," Denny said. "That's all I can give you now."

Denny tossed his cell phone onto the seat beside him and turned on his truck, struggling to slow his spinning thoughts and the dread hovering at the center of them.

For a brief and blessed moment his life had had a solid and stable focus. For a moment he had dared to envision a future with Evangeline and Ella.

Once again his life was dumped upside down. Once again he had to plan on the fly.

Only this time he felt as if more was at stake.

He drove home in a daze, trying to think. Trying to plan.

He didn't even mind that as soon as he got home Olivia and Trista gave him a quick progress report on Ella, who was napping, and then took off. He didn't want to talk to anyone.

He dropped onto the worn recliner and looked around the room that held some wonderful moments. Was it only last week he had sat in that love seat with Evangeline, pretending to watch a movie when all he could think about was her? He had dared to make plans the past few days, feeling fairly confident she felt the same way about him. He was thinking marriage.

But now?

What could he possibly offer her? Debt and

struggling and a life of wondering if they could make ends meet. He thought of the clothes she wore, the car she drove. The things she liked. Behind all that he saw Tyler and his perfect clothes and obvious wealth.

He knew Evangeline wasn't shallow or materialistic but at the same time, he couldn't begin to provide for her on the level she was accustomed to.

But what else could he do? Walk away?

He massaged his temples, trying to think. To plan. Then finally he prayed.

"Lord, help me to make the right decision. I have Ella to think of now, as well. I have to do what's best for her, too."

He spent the rest of Ella's nap time sitting at the kitchen table with his calculator and a pad of paper, scribbling figures, adding, subtracting and budgeting. If he sold the trucks he would have enough money to make a down payment, but it would mean a large debt load and a reduced income to pay it with. If he kept the trucks to help make the payments, he would have to work full-time, which meant the cows wouldn't get proper care, which would reduce the ranch income. If he sold the cows, he would lose that income, as well.

He could make it okay if he had five years to lease the ranch and build up his cow herd enough that he could sell the trucks and pay down whatever debt he would have to incur. It was a good plan, a solid plan, but it was a five-year plan that needed both the income from the ranch and the trucks to work.

Two hours and reams of paper later, reality hit him like a punch in his stomach.

There was no way he could buy out Andy right now. There was no way he could make this work.

There was no way he could give Evangeline the kind of life he wanted to offer her.

Evangeline laid the handset in the cradle and drummed her fingers on the counter. Denny still wasn't answering his phone nor had he replied to the two messages she had left this morning.

She walked to the front door and locked it. Late-afternoon sun slanted into the store, illuminating dust motes dancing on its beams. She turned off the low-key music she often played in the store and a heavy quiet descended.

Somehow, since Ella had moved to the ranch, the quiet seemed palpable and filled the store. A shiver tickled Evangeline's neck as she looked around.

Someday it would be hers. Someday.

But now that didn't matter. At one time the store had been all she had. Even when she was dating Tyler there had been an emptiness in the relationship that the store had filled.

But with Denny she felt as if her heart couldn't get any fuller. Couldn't hold any more happiness.

And she missed him.

Evangeline had stayed away Monday and Tuesday to give Denny a chance to catch up with his sisters. He hadn't called her but she wasn't surprised. Now that Olivia was here she knew he would be able to work a few more shifts on the gravel truck.

But still, she had hoped to hear something from him. It was now Wednesday and she wasn't sure what to do.

She could go upstairs to her quiet apartment or she could go to the ranch.

Her thoughts cast back to their date on Sunday and a smile curved her lips. Maybe he was waiting to hear from her?

With this in mind she ran the rest of the way up the stairs and took her time to pick out precisely the right outfit. Did her makeup just so. Wore her hair the way he said he liked it, hanging loose and free around her face.

Half an hour later she was pulling up to the ranch and parking beside Denny's truck, which was next to the beat-up old car that belonged to Olivia and Trista.

She stepped out of her vehicle, her heart lifting at the sight of the sun slanting down the hills and the cows grazing contentedly in the pasture.

Her thoughts ticked back to a scene so similar it made her heart ache.

Her father's cows in the pasture. Her mother calling her to come in for supper.

A sense of melancholy drifted over her but it was replaced by a happier thought.

Someday she might be living here again.

She took in a deep, cleansing breath, easing away the sadder memories. Then with a lift of her heart she walked over to the house.

She knocked lightly on the door and stepped inside. She heard voices. Loud voices, which made her pause.

"Does Evangeline know about this?" she heard Trista ask. "Are you going to tell her?"

Evangeline pressed her hand to her suddenly erratic heart, moving to one side of the door, out of view. Tell her what?

"Not yet," he replied. "I can't tell her yet."

"When will you?"

She should leave, she thought as a sense of impending doom hung over her at the sound of Denny's answering sigh.

But fear and worry kept her feet planted to the spot as she leaned back against the wall for support.

"I've finally connected with Lila's parents," Denny was saying, as if ignoring Trista's other question. "They're back from their trip and they said they could help me out. I just have to figure out what to do about the cows."

Lila's parents? What to do about the cows? What was Denny talking about?

"Uncle Ben said he knew of a place I could take them," Denny continued. "If I can't, I'll have to sell them before I leave."

His words thudded like a cleaver in her soul. Leave?

"So you'll keep the trucks when you go?" Trista asked.

"I'll take them with me. Leave a couple here to finish off this contract. They're what make me money. It's the only way I can get my stake together. I have to think about the future."

Evangeline stifled a sob at the words Denny used. The same ones her father always used. And now he was making the same choice her father always made.

Go to him. Tell him that you matter to him. Tell him you want to be involved in this decision.

Evangeline beat down the insidious voice. She had no claim to Denny or any input into his decisions. Besides, there was no way she was pleading or begging. She had done enough of that with her father. She had even come close to doing that with Tyler before she'd seen him with that other girl.

Dear Lord, I can't do this. I can't be left behind again.

Evangeline waited another moment, her feet rooted to the floor, clinging to a slim hope that Denny would say something that would change everything.

But all she heard was the clink of silverware and Ella's burbling voice.

Evangeline pressed her hand to the sharp pain in her heart. She was losing them both. Denny and Ella.

And he hadn't had the decency to tell her himself.

She dug down deep and pushed herself away from the wall, blindly stumbling over Denny's work boots.

She caught her headlong fall by grabbing the bench close to the door, but she'd misjudged the distance and fell to her knees.

"Who's there?" Denny called out.

Evangeline righted herself, scrambling to her feet. But just as she was about to reach for the door handle she felt Denny catch her by the arm.

"Evangeline. Are you okay?"

She was far from okay, but she wasn't telling him that.

Instead she gathered the few remnants of pride she had left, shook his hand off and turned to face him.

"I'm fine," she said, her voice cool.

"But your dress…"

Evangeline looked in the direction he was pointing, dismayed to see a large rip in the skirt of her favorite dress. The one her father had bought her the last time he had come rolling into town. Said he had bought it at some upscale store in the United States.

Not that it mattered what her dress looked like when her life felt torn from top to bottom.

"So, you're leaving?" Evangeline asked, holding her head high, her chin up, trying desperately not to cry like she had the first time she had seen Denny. When he had come to give her news of another disappointment in her life.

But this one hurt so much more.

"Is that why you didn't call me?" she challenged. "Because you're planning to leave?"

"I had too much to think about. Too much to organize."

"Was I somewhere on that list of things you had to organize?" she asked, unable to keep the challenging tone out of her voice.

The sudden frown on Denny's face showed her she was being dramatic again. But she didn't care. She had heard him. He had his plans in place.

Denny grabbed the back of his neck with his hand, pulling down. "Yes, I was going to talk to you. I just needed…" He sighed and looked at her. "I had a lot to organize. To plan."

"I'm sure you did." She grabbed the door handle, unable to keep up the pretense that her opinion mattered. That she had any part in his future. "I better let you get back to your plans."

"Evangeline. Wait. I can explain."

She stopped. "Explain what? Explain how you made all these plans without thinking I might want to be involved? Explain how you are leaving?"

Exactly like her father always left?

"It's for a while. Just until—"

"You get your stake together." Evangeline released a harsh laugh, repeating the words he'd spoken only minutes ago. She had heard this too often.

No. This time she would be in charge. This time she would be the one leaving.

"You know what? Let's forget it," she said. "I don't want you to feel you have to involve me in your plans and I'm thinking you're not the right person for me, after all." She felt her words spilling out of a place of hurt and pain and a history of disappointment. But she couldn't stop them. "I don't think this would have worked."

Stop. Stop.

But Evangeline didn't listen to the voice of reason. She was beyond that.

"So I guess this is goodbye," she said.

And then, before he saw her tears fall, she turned and ran toward her car. She got in and as she drove away she glanced in her rearview mirror.

Denny wasn't even watching her leave.

She looked ahead, barely able to see the road through the tears filling her eyes. She blinked them away as sobs gathered like a storm in her chest.

What had she done? What had she said?

The truth. Denny was leaving. And he hadn't bothered to let her know why or to ask her for her input. She didn't matter as much to him as she'd thought.

Somehow she made it back to the store. Once inside she ran up the stairs to her bedroom, where she dropped onto the bed, letting the tears and sorrow overtake her.

And with them, reality.

Denny was no hero, after all.

Denny was just like her father.

"You need to go after her." Olivia stood with her hands on her hips, glaring at Denny as he gathered up the dishes from dinner. He had been busy all evening sorting out his cows, trying to decide which ones to ship and which ones could go to his uncle's ranch, so dinner had been late.

Trista had left yesterday for a job interview and Olivia had taken Ella for a long walk. They had gotten back just when Denny had returned from a day of truck driving.

Of course he'd had to make supper. At least Olivia had washed Ella up, fed her and put her to bed.

"You need to talk to her," Olivia continued, hugging her knees against her chest.

"And say what? Come away with me and be my beloved and live in a broken-down trailer while I'm gone for fourteen hours a day driving a gravel truck?" Denny snapped as he rinsed off the dishes. "Oh, yeah, and take care of my kid from another woman? Be a part of my disaster of a life?" Denny clenched his fists on the counter, stopping the flow of angry words.

"You might have given her the chance to think about it," Olivia retorted.

Denny had entertained that thought a number of times. But he didn't know if Evangeline's feelings for him were strong enough to withstand the scrimping and scraping type of life he could offer her. And he couldn't put himself through that again. Because seeing Evangeline leave would devastate him in a way that Lila's leaving never had.

No. It was better this way.

Not much better, but at least he hadn't made a

fool of himself by declaring undying love to her before she'd said goodbye to him. This way he could leave with some measure of pride.

"You don't know what you're talking about," Denny said, growing quiet as he started setting the dishes in the dishwasher. "I have Ella to think about now. I can't complicate my life any further. And you heard her. You heard her tell me it's over."

He hadn't wanted to dwell on Evangeline's angry words. On one level it made leaving easier.

But on a deeper one they'd rent his soul and heart in two.

Olivia didn't reply and Denny hoped the subject was closed. Thankfully, Trista had kept quiet about the matter. She seemed to understand, better than Olivia, what Denny had to deal with.

"And you don't mind leaving Ella with Lila's parents?"

"They're good people. I know they'll take care of her."

"But they're not her father."

"You think I want to leave Ella with Lila's parents?" Denny asked, grabbing the box of dishwashing soap and dumping some into the dispenser. "You think it isn't killing me to think of leaving that little ragamuffin with someone else while I head out for days at a time?" Never mind thinking of Evangeline, who was now out of his life.

"But there has to be another way," Olivia said.

Denny was quiet a moment. "You could help."

She released a tight laugh. "Sorry. I can't."

"Of course you can't." As soon as the words left his mouth he regretted his harsh tone. He had always been there for his sisters. For once he wished they could be there for him.

"I'm not in any position to do anything for anyone else" was her enigmatic reply. "Maybe later."

"I don't need later. I need now." Denny shut the dishwasher and started it up.

"Trista has that job she's heading for in a week. Adrianna is still gone. And who knows where Nate is," Olivia replied.

"Whichever cutting horse competition is going right now," Denny said. "Not that I could count on that loner to stick his neck out for a kid."

Denny sighed then as he heard Ella rustling around in the crib, and his heart contracted. He had come to love that little girl with a love so deep it scared him. He had promised himself he wouldn't let anyone close, but she had ingrained herself in his heart.

Her and Evangeline.

The thought of Evangeline created a twist of sorrow so strong, he almost groaned.

Evangeline. The woman who filled a space

in his heart that no woman had. He had lost her, but he had to try to find some way to keep Ella.

"So what are you going to do? You can't stay here," Olivia said.

"That much is obvious." Denny took in a long, slow breath. "I don't want to talk about this now. I have a hundred phone calls to make."

"I'm going for a walk," Olivia said.

"I need you to stay with Ella."

"I spent the whole day with her," Olivia returned. "I need a few moments to myself."

Then, without a backward glance, she walked out the door.

Denny blew out his breath and shoved his hands through his hair. Just once he wished things would go his way, he thought, feeling a stab of self-pity.

As soon as the thought formulated he pushed it back. He had problems to deal with, and dwelling on his bad luck wouldn't help. And he had to keep himself busy.

It was the only way he could keep thoughts of Evangeline safely tucked away in the furthest reaches of his mind.

Chapter Fourteen

"'The Lord is good to those whose hope is in Him, to the one who seeks Him....'" Evangeline ran her fingers over the words of Lamentations, letting their truth soak into her soul. She had been reading her Bible more regularly of late and somehow Lamentations seemed to speak to her, especially that passage.

"Please forgive me," she prayed, closing her eyes. "Forgive me for not putting my hope in You. For thinking I can find happiness in other places than in Your presence. Forgive me for not putting You first in my life."

As they had for the past three pain-filled and empty days, her thoughts skipped back to Denny and that horrible moment at the ranch.

Any number of times she had reached for the phone to call him, but stopped herself. He was the one at fault. He was the one who didn't think she needed to be consulted. He was the one who made all the decisions. He was the one who was leaving.

She wasn't giving him any more power than he already had. It was the right thing to do, she had reasoned.

Then why did it hurt so much?

She covered her face with her hands, stifling a sob. She had been brokenhearted when she'd first met Denny. She should be used to it.

But this was far worse. Because while she and Tyler had been dating for years, in some corner of her mind she'd intrinsically known their relationship wasn't built on anything lasting.

Tyler was romantic. Attractive. He'd had a good job and done all the right things. Brought her flowers and expensive gifts, taken her to the best restaurants.

And yet, it wasn't until she'd started spending time with Denny that she'd realized what had been missing with Tyler.

Sincerity. Humanity. Selfless giving. And a simple faith in God.

So why had Denny done this to her?

Evangeline pushed herself up from her chair and, restless, walked down the stairs to the store. It was late evening and the security lamp at the back of the store shed a weak, pale light over the wooden floors, casting shadows across the bookshelves that mingled with the shadows from the streetlights outside. Evangeline had spent these past few nights here, taking inventory, rearranging books and creating new displays, trying to keep busy.

For so much of her life the store had been her everything. But now it was simply a building that held a booming emptiness left by Denny and Ella's departure.

She knew he hadn't left yet. Renee and Mia kept her updated even though she didn't ask. Thankfully they'd sensed she didn't want to talk about Denny though she had seen a question in Renee's eyes more than once.

She stopped at the children's section, thinking of the plans she had been so excited about a couple of months ago. The plans she would implement when her father signed the store over to her. That idea had consumed her life at one time. Now it didn't seem so important.

She looked around the store once more. There was nothing to do here unless she wanted to rearrange the sections one more time in a useless bid to keep her mind occupied. She was about to go back up the stairs when the sound of footsteps reverberated in the hallway.

Who could be here? Who had a key to that door?

Her heart leaped in her throat. Denny.

Her feet barely touched the floor as she ran through the back room. A sliver of light shone out from under the door leading to the hallway.

She yanked it open in time to see a man inserting a key into the door of the apartment. Not much taller than her, he wore blue jeans, a wool sweater and a straw fedora.

Not Denny.

And as she caught the faintest whiff of cherry tobacco she realized who it was.

Her father.

He looked up as Evangeline's heart quieted in her chest and she found her breath.

"Hey, sweetie. Didn't think you would be in the store," Andy said, straightening and walking toward her.

Evangeline's heart twisted as she rearranged her expectations and reactions.

"Daddy" was all she could say.

Then, in spite of his absences and the accumulation of disappointments of the past few years, she ran to him and let him enfold her in the shelter of his arms. She pressed her face against the rough wool of his sweater, inhaling the smell of his pipe tobacco, letting her thoughts slip back to happier times.

For a moment she felt her sorrow overtake her and a sob crawl up her throat. Her dad was here. He would make everything better.

But then reality intruded and Evangeline pulled away from her father's embrace. Her dad had probably come because he needed something.

"So, what brings you back here?" she asked, disappointed at the faint trembling of her words.

"You, of course." His voice held a note of hurt. "I told you I would come."

Evangeline only nodded, still trying to adjust her emotions. "Do you want some tea or coffee?"

"Coffee would be great. I've been driving all day."

She gave him a quick smile then walked back into the bookstore, flicking on a few lights as she went.

"Wow. Looks good in here," he said, pausing by the back of the store to look around. "I like the new displays."

"I've been busy."

"So where were you putting that kid's corner you were talking about?"

"Over there, beside the cash register." Evangeline pressed her lips together, a painful yearning gripping her at the memory of Ella toddling around that corner of the store, waving a rattle and laughing at the sound, sitting on the floor stacking cardboard boxes on top of each other.

When Denny had decided to leave, he'd broken her heart twice. Once for him and once for Ella.

"It's a great idea, poppet," Andy said approvingly. "What were you planning to do here?"

"Why don't we talk about that over a cup of coffee?"

Her father shot her a puzzled look that Evangeline ignored. She fought down her resentment at her father's blithe attitude. He didn't know what had just happened, she reminded herself. The last time they had talked she was full of plans for the store he was to sign over to her.

She had been so excited at that time.

Those expectations seemed like years ago instead of mere weeks. So much had happened to shift her expectations of life and love in that time.

She banished the thoughts and strode up the stairs, her father slowly following her.

A few minutes later she had a plate of cookies set out for him and a cup of coffee.

"Did you make these yourself?" he asked as he dunked one in his steaming mug.

Evangeline nodded. One of the many things she had kept herself busy with the past few days.

"I used Mom's recipe," she said as she pulled a chair up across the table from him.

She didn't imagine the flicker of pain that crossed his face when she'd said that and she repressed a momentary frustration. All these years and the mention of her mother still created this reaction?

"So, how long are you back for?" she asked, wrapping her hands around the warm mug of coffee she had poured for herself.

"Couple of weeks. I've got some work to do." He gave her a bright smile. "Tomorrow you and I are going to see Zach Truscott. I made an appointment to sign the store over."

Older longings and yearnings made her heart quicken at the thought. But only for a moment. She would have the bookstore.

But not Denny.

She would end up like her aunt, alone and a spinster, living above a bookstore.

She shook the morbid thought off, trying to realize that what her father was giving her was an opportunity. An answer to older prayers.

"That's great," she said, trying to inject the necessary enthusiasm into her voice. "Really great. I'm glad."

Her father's frown told her that her feigned attempt at excitement had fallen flat.

And the award for poorest reaction goes to me, she thought.

"You don't sound glad," he said.

"I am. I really am." That was a touch more realistic, but still not the reaction he would have gotten a few months ago.

"I've got a few irons in the fire that will make

it easier to hand the store over," he said, sounding heartier than she felt.

She didn't really want to know about another of his schemes, but not asking would smack of ingratitude. And she was grateful. Truly she was.

As a single girl she would have to find a way to make a living in this world. The bookstore would give her a good one if she was able to implement her plans.

"So what are you working on now?" she asked.

He leaned forward, his eyes shining. "It's a great opportunity, poppet. A chance to get a decent stake together," he said, using words so familiar to Evangeline that she smiled.

"What's the opportunity?" she asked, going through the motions of being interested. Just as she always did when her father started on yet another scheme.

"Real estate. Down in Arizona. Stuff is going dirt cheap and me and my buddy are looking at a couple of fantastic deals. The economy will pick up. I know it will, and then, boom, I'll be in the money, honey." He slapped the table with an open palm for emphasis, almost making Evangeline jump.

"That's good," she said slowly.

"It's solid, poppet. Rock solid."

"And how are you getting the money you need for this?"

"I'm selling the ranch."

"I know that, but you won't have that money for about five years."

Her father took a quick sip of his coffee then shook his head. "Nope. I'm getting it sooner than that. I put the ranch up for sale now. I've got a couple of buyers who are interested. They're coming up in the next few days. That's why I'm here."

Evangeline stared at her father as confusing phrases spun through her brain. "Buyers? Coming up? But I thought Denny..." She shook her head as if to rearrange the words he had thrown at her. "I thought Denny was buying it?"

"Can't afford it. He said he had a five-year plan and though a few things had changed, he couldn't do it. So now I've got a few other people interested and he's packing up and leaving. Which is funny. Last time I talked to him he told me that he'd met someone. Was looking at settling down."

Met someone? Settling down?

Had Denny been talking about Ella?

Or her?

Her thoughts circled around each other, trying to settle as her father, all fired up on caffeine and sugar, kept talking.

"Now he's telling me to find someone else to buy the place. He can't afford it. Doesn't want to go that deep into debt. So I made a few calls to other people I knew were interested in land in the area and they're coming out. Shame about Denny, though. I figured he'd like the place enough to take a few chances on it, but he said he couldn't."

Her heart danced against her rib cage as the events of the past week coalesced. Though she was still upset with Denny for not involving her in the process, she now had more information as to why.

"So you wanted your money right away from the ranch? What about the lease you had with Denny?"

Her father looked down at his coffee, looking shamefaced. "It was just a handshake agreement. Nothing written down."

She felt a flush of momentary shame at her father's cavalier dismissal of something Denny had counted on. "That doesn't sound very gentlemanly," she said with a note of reprimand. "What did Denny say to that?"

"He was great about it. Told me it was ultimately my place and that he knew he didn't have any right to make demands."

Evangeline sat back in her chair, still trying to absorb what her father had told her.

"Said he was leaving a couple of his trucks behind to finish the contract and was selling his cows," her father continued, his words rushing out of him. "Poor guy. I feel bad for him. He was so glad he could buy back some of the cows from his old ranch, which he had to sell when he got divorced. Told me it was like he could keep his parents' legacy. And he's got that kid and all, and he said that he had to think of her…."

He sighed, quiet a moment as if acknowledging Denny's dilemma with a few moments of silence. But it was merely a pittance of time because seconds later he looked up, bright-eyed and excited again. "But, hey, this is such a great chance for me. A super chance. I'll do great, and even better, I can sign the bookstore over to you."

"And when you get the money?" Evangeline said, ignoring his repetition of his big plans for her life.

"I got my plans, got my dreams," he said. "I'm out of here."

"Why?"

Her quiet question stopped the flow of words. He cut his gaze away, looking out the window overlooking the town. The streetlights cast golden cones over the darkened street. A few cars drove by, their headlights flashing.

"I can't be here. Every time I come home… I think of your mother." His voice broke just enough to create an answering thrum of sympathy.

But only for a moment.

"And what about me? I've stayed here, missing mom, as well. And on top of that, missing you."

Her father sent her a pained look and reached across the table to catch her hand. "I love you, you know that, but I can't be here. It hurts too much."

Evangeline's mind tripped back to one of her first memories of Denny. A reluctant father.

But following that, the reality of how he had coped. How he had rearranged his life to take care of Ella. How he made everything about her.

And another thought struck deep in her soul.

Denny was nothing like her father, after all.

She stared at her father a moment, thinking, trying to rearrange her perceptions. Her thoughts.

Then she knew what she had to do.

She leaned forward. "Dad, how much money would you get from the ranch?"

"You know what it is worth."

"Sort of. But would you get the same amount if you sold the bookstore?"

"Sell the bookstore?" Her father looked surprised. "Why would I do that? It's yours. It's for you. Always was."

Not always, Evangeline thought, but she pushed that petty thought back. "Just tell me."

Her father leaned back in his chair, his arms crossed over his chest as he seemed to consider this.

"It wouldn't be as much, but real estate in downtown Hartley Creek is pretty primo especially because I own the building outright. I've had a few people interested but it was always for you, poppet, so I told them no."

"But you have some loans against the ranch yet."

He shrugged that comment aside. "Not that much, but I guess if I pay them out, what the store would bring would come close to the same."

She nodded, her heart thudding against her chest wall. A moment of indecision clutched at her but then she thought of Denny. Thought of all he had lost. Thought of Ella and the sacrifices Denny had made for her.

"Because I want you to sell the bookstore. I want you to use that money to finance your scheme."

Her father only stared at her. "But, poppet, you can't afford to buy the store."

She waved off his objections. "I know. And it doesn't matter."

"So why are you doing this? This store is all you've ever wanted."

It was. But now that she didn't have Denny and Ella in her life anymore, it didn't seem as important. The bookstore had been a large part of her life and now as her deepest wish was about to come true, she realized she had clung to the bookstore for the wrong reasons. It had become the focus of her life. It had become a way to keep her father connected to her when, in reality, her father would never be the father she had hoped he would be. He would never settle down here.

And, somehow, it didn't matter as much.

If she gave up the bookstore, Denny could keep the ranch. He could take care of Ella and give Ella the kind of childhood Evangeline had had for only a few short years.

It was for Ella, she told herself as she told her father again that this was what she wanted to do. It was all for Ella.

But later, as she lay in her bed, her heart lonely and aching, she knew it was more for Denny.

The next day the sun hid behind clouds and rain drizzled down. The bookstore seemed gloomy and dull and as Evangeline watched the water slide down the large front windows of the store she felt a chill slowly seep into her soul.

She leaned her elbows on the counter and idly paged through a book she had just received in a shipment this morning.

Most of the boxes sat in the back room, where book club was held, still unopened.

Evangeline had only opened the box of books she had ordered for the book club. She wished she could cancel. She wasn't in the mood.

And the book they had decided on was too depressing. Something Jeff Deptuck had campaigned for. An Arctic expedition gone wrong and the repercussions for a man and his family back home in England.

She leaned her elbows on the counter, suddenly tired. The morning had been unusually busy, which was good, and right now it was lunchtime. In half an hour she was to meet her father and Zach Truscott at Mug Shots to talk about the sale of the store. Evangeline wanted to make sure that her father kept to his side of the bargain and part of that was to draw up a legal lease agreement for Denny.

She shivered, wrapping the soft cashmere sweater her father had given her this morning around her shoulders. At first she'd wanted to refuse. But the reality was that this was her father's way of expressing his affection for her and she was at a low point in her life. Ready to take any expression of caring.

So she'd put it on.

But the soft wool and the pale yellow color did nothing to brighten her low spirits.

I miss him. I miss Denny.

Her heart clenched at the thought.

Then she closed her eyes, slapped the book shut and straightened. She had to get over this.

Her life was about to make some major changes and that was a good thing.

Change was as good as a rest. Maybe she had stayed in Hartley Creek, waiting, too long. Maybe it was time she ventured out and figured out what she wanted. Make some plans and schemes of her own.

She lifted her chin, ready to take on her new life when the door to the bookstore opened.

A man, silhouetted against the gloom behind him, paused inside the frame. Tall, with broad shoulders, lean hips.

And a cowboy hat that dripped water onto the floor of the store.

Icy fingers clutched at her heart and Evangeline pressed a hand against her chest as if to contain the chill.

"What…what can I do for you?" she stammered as the man stepped farther into the store, sweeping his dripping hat off his head.

Denny stood in front of her, his jaw shadowed with stubble, his eyes bleary. He blinked a moment, as if coming back from a dark place into light, then he took another tentative step toward her.

"I was just talking to your father," he said.

Evangeline could only nod as she ran her suddenly damp palms down the sides of her skirt.

"He told me about the store."

Another nod as she struggled with what to say to a man who had once held her heart in hands that now worked their way around the brim of a dripping cowboy hat.

"Why are you selling it?" he asked.

Evangeline swallowed, then licked her dry lips. "I think you know why."

Denny nodded. "I think I do, too, but I'd like to hear it from you."

"Why? So you can make another decision without me?"

"Evangeline—"

"No. You don't get to act as if you're in charge here. I'm in charge. I'm the one who decided to sell the store. And if you really must know, I did it for Ella."

He blanched at that and Evangeline felt suddenly remorseful. He nodded slowly, as if understanding. "Of course you did. That's amazing of you. I knew you were a selfless person. I'm not surprised."

She waited a moment, still unsure of what to say and what she was allowed to expect.

"Why didn't you tell me you were leaving?" she asked, resting her hands on the counter as if finding support there. "Why didn't you think I needed to know?"

Denny bit his lip, as if thinking, then looked up at her, his eyes narrowed. "I didn't tell you because I was ashamed. Because once your father wanted to sell the ranch it meant I had to go back to the kind of life I had before. And I didn't want that for you. I wanted the best for you. A home. A stable living. I wanted to be able to support you. And once I knew I couldn't give you that, I couldn't…I couldn't…" His sentence faded away but his eyes held hers.

"Did you really think I needed so much?"

Denny gave her a weary smile and lifted his chin toward her. "Look at you. I don't know much about clothes but I can tell quality. Everything you have, everything you wear, is the best. Expensive and beautiful. I can't give that to you now and I certainly couldn't give that to you if I had to leave. I couldn't even offer you a decent home. Maybe a rented double-wide at best while I was off driving a truck and you were scrabbling to pay bills. Lila couldn't live that life—"

"I'm not Lila," she protested, hurt that he assumed she was such a princess. "I care about you and I would be willing to make sacrifices to be with you. I'm not a diva and I'm not high maintenance. I know how to make sacrifices for love. That's why I told my father to sell this store. So you could keep the ranch. I did it because I love you."

She stopped herself then, clapping her hand

over her mouth as if to hold back the words already lying between them.

It was too late to backtrack and the shock on his face showed her he'd heard every word.

"You gave up this bookstore for me?"

"And Ella." Then she shrugged, realizing he needed to hear the full truth. "But mostly for you."

Denny walked over slowly, as if engaged in a showdown. But he didn't stop at the counter. He came around it, dropped his hat to the floor and caught her by the shoulders.

"You love me?"

Evangeline felt exposed and vulnerable but she figured she might as well see this through. "Yes. I do."

Denny looked down at her, his eyes holding a warmth that kindled an answering glow in her own soul. "I love you, Evangeline. I have loved you for a while now."

She felt her heart quiver at the fervent note in his voice.

Then he pulled her close, his arms damp from the rain outside, his lips cool. Their kiss warmed them both.

He pulled away, but cradled her head against his shoulder, resting his chin on her hair as he took in a long, slow breath.

"I love you so much," he murmured. "I can't

believe you would do that. That you would sacrifice what you loved because of me. No one has
ever done anything like that for me. Ever."

She had no answer to that so she wrapped her
arms around him and held him close.

He loved her and she loved him. For now, that
was enough.

They stood that way for a while, then Denny
slowly stepped back, his rough fingertips gently
tracing her features. Her eyebrows, her cheeks,
her lips, her chin, as if trying to memorize her.

He kissed her again, smiling. "But I can't let
you do that," he said. "I can't let you make that
sacrifice."

"But you have to," she said, holding his eyes.
"Not to get all practical, but I know you can't afford to buy out my father."

"I can't. And I have wanted more than anything to give you a home on the ranch, the place
you grew up. I was making dreams and plans
about us."

"You were?" she asked, his words lighting a
candle of wonder in her soul.

"Of course. You were the reason for all the decisions I was making. But now..." Denny sighed
lightly and looked as if he was about to argue
with her. "I can't let you do this."

"Don't you understand?" she said, catching
hold of his arms. "I want to be with you. And if

that means selling the bookstore, then I'm happy to do it. This way you don't have to leave and I don't have to leave and we can be on the ranch, the place I grew up. The place I had my happiest memories. We can make new and better ones, and that means more to me than keeping the bookstore."

Denny's eyes locked with hers as a smile of amazement crawled over his lips. "You mean that, don't you?"

"I do. I love you and I want to be with you and I want you to be happy and I want me to be happy and this way…this way everybody is happy. You have all I have ever wanted. You have a loyal, faithful heart. A heart for family."

Denny laughed but Evangeline could see he still harbored some doubts and concerns. "I come with a lot more family than you might be comfortable with."

"I'm willing to risk it." She stopped herself there. She had said enough. It was up to Denny now.

Then the door to the bookstore opened again and Evangeline felt a beat of exasperation. Didn't people know she was planning her future here?

But as the door shut behind the newest customer, Evangeline's heart thudded in her chest.

Her father stood just inside the door, looking

at Denny and Evangeline with narrowed eyes, as if trying to adjust to this reality.

"So. This is the guy you're willing to give your dream up for?"

Evangeline's heart slowed, then she nodded. "This bookstore isn't as important to me as Denny is."

"He must be special."

Evangeline looked back at Denny but his eyes were on her father. Holding her hand, he turned to face him. "Before I say anything more to Evangeline, I want you to know that I want to ask her to marry me."

Evangeline felt her breath leave her chest as Denny shot her a sidelong glance.

"If you'll have me, that is."

She clung to his hand with both of hers, her chest unable to hold in the happiness that made her heart want to burst. "Of course."

"Are you asking my permission?" Andy said, walking toward them, still frowning.

"I guess I'm letting you know what my intentions are," Denny said.

Andy looked at Denny then back at Evangeline. "So, poppet, is he the one? Is he the hero you've always been waiting for?"

"And more," Evangeline said, unable to say more than that.

Andy released a heavy sigh then turned to Denny. "You know that she's precious to me."

"And she's precious to me," Denny said, turning his attention back to Evangeline, his eyes shining with a light that stirred her to the depths of her soul. "And I hope to take care of her the best way that I can."

"Okay. If that's the way it is." Andy walked toward them and laid his hand on each of their shoulders. "Then you have my blessing." He squeezed Evangeline's shoulder. "I haven't always been a good father to you," he said quietly. "But I hope I can be the father I should be right now. I want you both to know I'm not selling the ranch or the bookstore."

His words tugged Evangeline's attention away from Denny.

"What do you mean?"

Andy gave her a melancholy smile. "I'm sorry, poppet. For all that I put you through. But I see that you really care for this guy. I can't imagine you giving up something so important to you if he wasn't the one." He reached over and tucked a strand of hair behind her ear. "I want you to be happy and if this is what it takes, then I'm willing to give up a few plots and plans to see that happen."

Evangeline returned his hug. "Thanks, Daddy" was all she could say.

Andy gave her a quick nod, then took a step back. "So, I guess I'll leave you two alone. I'm sure you have lots to talk about."

Denny smiled down at Evangeline, slipping his arm around her shoulders. "We certainly do."

Andy gave them both a smile, then turned and walked out of the store.

Evangeline waited until the door fell shut behind him and turned back to Denny. "I can't believe this is happening."

"Me, either. But I want you to know that I will spend my lifetime loving you and taking care of you."

"I know you will."

This netted her another quick kiss.

"So, anything else you need to do here?" Denny said. "I'd like to go home."

Home. The word filled her soul, soothing away years of sorrow and pain.

"That sounds like a good plan," she said. And on their way out of the store, Evangeline picked out a book for Ella. Tucking it under her arm, she slipped her hand in Denny's and together they walked out of the store and toward the next part of their story.

* * * * *

Dear Reader,

I love bookstores. I love spending time in them and the expectations they create every time I step in one. The sense that all these books so neat and clean and uncracked hold an adventure waiting for me. I used to want to own a bookstore just so I could read brand-new books instead of the well-read ones I got from our local library. My own house is a reflection of that wish. Bookshelves line the walls of two rooms and part of our living room. I love buying books and with this story of Evangeline and her own bookstore I was able to live out part of my fantasy. But the most important book, the most read book in our home is our Bible. From its pages we find our strength, our hope for our present and our future. I hope you too can find time to read that precious book and I hope you enjoyed this time with Evangeline and her bookstore.

Blessings,

Carolyne Aarsen

P.S. I love to hear from my readers. You can write to me at caarsen@xplornet.com or check out my website at www.carolyneaarsen.com. Be sure to sign up for my newsletter and be able to keep up with what is happening.

Questions for Discussion

1. Evangeline spent a lot of time waiting for her father. Was she realistic in her expectations of him? Why do you think he kept disappointing her?

2. Denny said that his life was messy. Why do you think he would say that?

3. Denny felt like he made some bad choices in his life. What were some of those choices and what were the repercussions for him and his family?

4. Not too many people get babies dropped into their life. How do you think you would react if this happened to you?

5. Evangeline had good friends to help her through the disappointments in her life. What role do your friends play in your life?

6. Evangeline is also part of a book club. Do you belong to one? If so, what kind of books do you read? If not, what would you like to read?

7. Tyler was part of Evangeline's past and maybe not the best part. Why do you think she might have been attracted to him?

8. Denny had his life all planned out—at least until Ella was dropped on his doorstep. I'm sure there have been many times in your life that plans have had to change because of circumstances beyond your control. How did you cope? How did it affect your relationship with God?

9. Why did Evangeline feel as if she had no input in Denny's decision when we know he meant a lot to her? What in her past might have made her feel that way? How did she resolve this?

10. Evangeline had a complicated relationship with her father. What do you think she needed to learn about him and about herself and about her relationship with God to truly accept who she was?